OUTCASTS OF
RIVER FALLS

∞

Other books by Jacqueline Guest

Belle of Batoche
Ghost Messages

JACQUELINE GUEST

OUTCASTS OF RIVER FALLS

∞

SEQUEL TO
BELLE OF BATOCHE

www.coteaubooks.com

© Jacqueline Guest, 2012

Edited by Laura Peetoom
Cover designed by Jamie Olson
Interior designed and typeset by Susan Buck
Printed and bound in Canada

Library and Archives Canada Cataloguing in Publication

Guest, Jacqueline
     Outcasts of River Falls : sequel to Belle of Batoche / Jacqueline Guest.

For ages 8-12.
ISBN 978-1-55050-480-4

     I. Title.

PS8563.U365O88 2012   jC813'.54   C2012-900428-6

Library of Congress Control Number 2012932997

2517 Victoria Avenue
Regina, Saskatchewan

Canada   S4P 0T2
www.coteaubooks.com

10 9 8 7 6 5 4 3 2 1

Available in Canada from:
Publishers Group Canada
2440 Viking Way
Richmond, British Columbia
Canada   V6V 1N2

Available in the US from:
Orca Book Publishers
www.orcabook.com
1-800-210-5277

Coteau Books gratefully acknowledges the financial support of its publishing program by: the Saskatchewan Arts Board, the Canada Council for the Arts, the Government of Canada through the Canada Book Fund, the Government of Saskatchewan through the Creative Economy Entrepreneurial Fund, the Association for the Export of Canadian Books and the City of Regina Arts Commission.

To the unsung Métis heroes of generations past
who had the foresight to recognise that
with hard work, fortitude and the unwillingness
to be defeated, a brighter future could be won
for their children.

Chapter 1

SECRETS FROM THE GRAVE

The ground shook and the wooden boards beneath Kathryn Tourond's feet groaned. She cringed as the sound of a thousand hissing dragons surrounded her and the world disappeared in a swirling fog of gauzy white mist.

As the roaring quieted and the choking steam that cloaked the train platform cleared, Kathryn saw a figure hurrying toward her. "About time," she grumbled, hefting her bulky carpet bag.

"Whew! I'm so sorry for my tardiness," the burnished skinned woman apologized as she patted down the strands of glossy black hair flying loose from her long braid. "I had some arrangements to make and then decided not to bring my usual transportation as it would be too small which meant hitching Nellie to the old Red River cart and that stubborn horse simply wasn't in the mood to cooperate. I'd hoped to be here long before you arrived." She paused long enough to smile. "It's indeed as Burns wrote, *the best laid schemes o' mice an' men...*"

The literary reference coming from someone obviously of the less fortunate classes surprised Kathryn. She eyed the homespun dress dubiously. It was clean and the cut impeccable, and yet so faded the blue flower print was barely there.

Kathryn smoothed the folds on her own fashionable frock, the deep burgundy taffeta deliberately chosen to show off her delicate coloring. Picking a miniscule piece of lint from her beautiful dress, she flicked it onto the worn wood beneath her feet. The plan was to look particularly perfect when she met her aunt, Miss Belle Tourond, for the first time and, modesty aside, she'd succeeded spectacularly.

The woman waited expectantly and it occurred to Kathryn that Aunt Belle must have sent an Indian maid to rescue her from this horrid station in the middle of the bald Alberta prairie. Of course, that would make sense. Someone as important as her aunt would have domestics for errands like fetching visitors from the train.

At that moment, the nun who had accompanied Kathryn on the four-day train ride from her home in Toronto came out of the station office and strode up to them.

"I'm Sister Bernadette, from Our Lady of Mercy Academy for Young Ladies." Her thunderous voice boomed out across the rolling grassland as she vigorously shook the maid's hand. "And this is Miss Kathryn Tourond. First, let me say how sorry I am for your loss... *tsk, tsk, tsk.*"

Kathryn flinched. That disapproving sound had annoyed her for the entire trip as she'd endured reprimands for the many minor sins committed on the journey. Everyone at school knew that nuns didn't approve of much, but during this adventure, it had become apparent that Sister Bernadette had taken that line of attack to the extreme. The stern Sister would make a wonderful Wicked Witch and Kathryn had always suspected there was a broomstick hidden somewhere beneath those voluminous robes.

Sister Bernadette wagged her head, making the long black veil on her habit sway ponderously back and forth. "The illness was tragic. For this young girl, only fourteen years old, to be left orphaned. I'm not sure if you were aware that her mother died when Kathryn was quite young – and now, her dear father, who did the right thing by sending the girl to us for her education, to be taken by consumption.... He made his wishes known to Mother Superior that if anything happened to him, she was to be sent to you. The entire thing is truly lamentable."

Kathryn was prepared to tolerate Sister's sharp tongue most of the time, however bringing up the circumstances of both her parents' deaths in front of this servant was unpardonable. It made that suffocating lump close Kathryn's throat and the tears that waited, hiding behind her self-control, threatened to spill over once again.

Biting her lip, she refused to give in to the grief. Her so-called *friends* at the academy had all watched, whispering behind her back, as they waited for her to make a spectacle of herself. Those petty tongue-waggers knew she was without *resources*, which always meant money, and had to leave the private school. When Kathryn heard the snickering, she'd resolved that the earth could crack open and swallow her whole before she'd let that pack of high-society hyenas see her cry.

Straightening her spine in a way that always made her feel in command of the situation, Kathryn hoped she appeared the very picture of the well-bred young lady she was as she threw a silencing dagger-glare at the talkative nun. Unfortunately, it missed its mark and the sister continued on relentlessly.

"We were so glad to discover our orphan girl had an aunt to take her in. We'd worried she would become a ward of the province. Thanks be to God and you, she now has a bright future with her family. I'm afraid there were some debts, *large* debts," the nun sniffed reprovingly. "Then the legal expenses and exorbitant train fare out here, *forty-two dollars*..." Here, her tone was filled with indignation at being charged such a scandalous amount. "All of which hasn't left much money for our poor, poor Kathryn."

Kathryn cringed at the word *poor* and her name being linked in the same sentence. And was the second 'poor' really necessary?

"The remaining money and the legal documents are in here." The nun held an envelope out to the native woman.

Kathryn's patience was at an end and her temper flared. What business was it of this maid's what her circumstances were? "Those documents, Sister, are for my aunt." She could feel her teeth clench as she attempted to wrestle the letter from the claw-like grip of the nun. "This servant...need not...bother...with them!" She pulled hard, yanking the envelope free.

Both women turned to Kathryn in surprise and Sister Bernadette's mouth actually dropped open in a very unattractive way.

"I thought you knew..." The nun's tone was full of pity, laced with what Kathryn could have sworn was a dash of smug satisfaction. "...This *is* your aunt."

"*My aunt!* Impossible!" The snort of derision slipped out before Kathryn had a chance to stop it. "Do I look like I could possibly be related to this woman? If you will notice, my hair is very blonde and I have a lovely pale pink complexion." She appraised the dark-skinned servant. "We could hardly be more dissimilar if we tried and besides, Aunt Belle is wealthy with a large, prosperous ranch and many head of cattle. My father told me this himself. She's a pillar of the community. Tell me Sister, could this woman be *that* aunt? She's a, a..." Kathryn fumbled for the right word.

The maid raised her chin and her dark eyes, so different from Kathryn's own green-flecked hazel, flashed a warning.

"The word you are searching for is *Métis*, and yes, I *am* your aunt. Your father obviously forgot to mention his ancestry while he was working for that high-priced company in Toronto and as to my social status – that too, was, shall we say, *exaggerated*."

Now it was Kathryn's turn to gape.

Chapter 2

WHITE KNIGHT NEEDED
APPLY WITHIN

After a jostling, bumping, bruising eternity, the noisy wooden cart crested a hill and spread out below Kathryn was a lush valley with tall trees and a wide river. The evening shadows spread sinuous purple fingers toward a scattering of dilapidated cabins edging the sides of the road. She shuddered. This must be where hobos and the down-and-out huddled in their tarpaper shanties. She turned about, expecting to see the gas streetlights of the town of Hopeful, Alberta, the town to which she had been banished.

"At last," the woman Kathryn now knew as Aunt Belle sighed, "journey's end."

Kathryn had a shiver of apprehension. "Journey's end? Surely, you can't mean those filthy shacks!"

"No, no, my dear." Aunt Belle gave the reins a shake to encourage the horse forward.

"Whew!" Kathryn relaxed. "You had me worried for a moment."

"My *filthy shack* is further back in the trees."

Kathryn gawked at her aunt in stunned silence. Was she expected to live in one of those tumble-down hovels? "Impossible!"

"Not at all," her aunt went on calmly. "Welcome to River Falls, Kathryn. We wanted the word 'river' in our name as rivers have always been important to the Métis. Here, we try to live close by each other so that we can help if needed. I'm a little further out, which isolates me some-what, however, it means I have the added blessing of being near to the river and in winter, that's wonderful indeed."

Still reeling at the news about the dismally sub-stan-dard housing, Kathryn had to ask. "Why would it matter if you live close to the river?"

Her aunt looked at her as though she were a very young child who knew nothing. "Hauling water is tough enough in the summer. Having to cut a hole in the ice and then drag the buckets to the house in a howling blizzard makes you pray the distance is short."

Kathryn was still confused; then the horror of it dawned. "You mean we don't have running water *inside* the house? How do you wash clothes? What about bathing and," she felt her cheeks grow hot, "and other bodily needs?'

They were passing the shacks now, and her aunt waved cheerily to several people who were outside chopping wood or tending gardens. Although her aunt had said these were Métis, Kathryn was surprised at how different they all appeared. There was a tall man with very dark skin and hair like her aunt, while another woman was blonder than Ingrid Svenson back at school and Ingrid was practically an albino!

As they rumbled by one particular boy, Kathryn noticed the outrageous hat that he wore. It was bright red and several sizes too large, with a long black raven's feather tucked roguishly into the band. As she stared, the impudent lad winked at her, then doffed the cap and made a sweeping bow. The gesture was so courtly she had the impulse to curtsey back. Ridiculously, he reminded her of the fairytale character *Puss-in-Boots*.

"I told you, dear," her aunt went on, bringing Kathryn's attention back to the dreadful conversation, "we haul water from the creek, and heat it for washing clothes or filling the bath. I keep the reservoir on the wood stove topped up for quick fixes." She laughed gently. "And for those other bodily needs... we have an outhouse."

"An *outhouse!* Kathryn Marie Tourond does not, not..." Kathryn's flustered brain searched for the right expression. *"Pee in a pit!"*

Her aunt was unperturbed. "Well, *Katy* Tourond will have to! In fact, that name suits a young Métis girl from River Falls. Yes, indeed, 'Katy' will do nicely."

"But, but..." Kathryn sputtered lamely. She was most certainly not a Katy, she was a Kathryn! She held her head up – Kathryn, regal and noble, like Catherine of Aragon, sad and courageous queen of Henry VIII. There were actually many similarities between her and the great queen – both exiled to a foreign land and having to live with – she shot her aunt a sidelong glance – unsuitable companions into whose alien world duty had thrust her.

A grasshopper landed on Kathryn's cheek, its hard wings frantically whirring. With a startled shriek, she batted the loathsome bug away, accidentally smacking her face in the process. Resuming her royal pose, she proffered a cold shoulder to her oblivious aunt, or as cold as one could get crammed together in a rickety Red River cart.

After meandering slowly through a grove of towering evergreens, they finally stopped in front of a small log cabin encircled by a wide veranda.

"Be it ever so humble...," Aunt Belle sighed. "Katy, you need to unload your trunk and carpet bag before I unhitch Nellie, then while you're taking everything into the house, I'll feed the old girl and put her away." She indicated a small lean-to near the cabin. Before Kathryn could correct her aunt on the insulting diminutive, Aunt Belle had climbed nimbly down, and was fussing with the tired nag – rubbing her wide muzzle, patting her corpulent flanks and cooing over the animal as though it were a particularly perfect specimen.

"What am I, the strong man from the circus?" Kathryn protested, to which the horse replied by noisily expelling a foul burst of noxious gas.

Choking, Kathryn hastily retreated to the back of the cart, offering her aunt some helpful advice. "I'm sure it would be a comfort to all in your River Falls if you took that flatulent beast to a veterinary surgeon!"

Aunt Belle paid little attention. "No money for that, Katy. Putting food on the table is enough of a battle."

Sizing up her baggage, Kathryn's anger was soon replaced with frustration. "How am I supposed to wrestle this into the house alone? There should be a porter to assist."

This time, her aunt appeared not to hear at all as she went about the process of disconnecting the horse from the cart. Kathryn waited, hoping for a hired man or at least a passer-by to haul the heavy cases. When no one came to her rescue, she knew she had no choice. Once her aunt unhitched the horse, the unstable Red River cart would tip forward, making the process of unloading even more odious.

Muttering obscenities to rival a sailor, Kathryn dropped her carpet bag to the ground, clambered down and undid the gate at the back of the cart. She felt very much like poor Cinderella, one of her favourite fairy tale heroines with whom she empathized completely, as she heaved on the large trunk holding her belongings. Shoving it out of the cart was torture; tugging it up the cabin steps simply beyond her.

The veranda sported a hanging swing, made of logs and rope. Kathryn climbed the steps; then, spreading her skirt evenly on each side of her as she liked, she sat to catch her breath while assessing her nemesis squatting so obstinately in the dirt.

What had she packed that was so heavy?

Then her lips crooked up. Of course! She'd packed twelve of the most essential things in life; those that she could not live without. She'd brought...her books.

Well, that made all the difference. "*Some rewards are worth the struggle,*" she breathed, reciting her personal motto. Standing, she resolutely attacked the trunk once more.

Finally, Kathryn manoeuvred the lumpish thing onto the covered porch. Opening the door, she dragged the cases and herself inside. Stretching her aching back, she surveyed the cabin. It was more spacious than it appeared from the outside; and, she admitted, far from being filthy, it was spotless.

Removing her bonnet, she laid it carefully on the trestle table to the right of the door. There were fresh wildflowers arranged in a chipped glass jar and she could smell the beeswax rubbed into the worn wood. Next to the table, a dressmaker's dummy stood at attention as it guarded an ancient treadle sewing machine. Kathryn wrinkled her nose at another unmistakable odour – that of lye soap, probably used to scrub the floors.

Across the cabin on the opposite wall, a wood-burning cook stove, dry sink with wash basin and two tall cupboards made up the kitchen area. Drying herbs hung from the rafters, their pungent smell wafting pleasantly to her. At the other end of the single room, a large stone fireplace made a grand statement indeed. To the right of the fireplace were two cozy overstuffed armchairs with a round table between and opposite these, a small horsehair settee sat as primly as a spinster at a shivaree.

Against the wall behind the chairs, a lovely old china cabinet, made by a reputable builder if Kathryn was any judge, sat in pride of place. It held what she imagined was the Sunday-best dishes. No doubt a cherished and irreplaceable treasure to be admired, yet never touched, perhaps brought out on special occasions such as Christmas dinner. She smiled indulgently; these country rubes were so quaint.

Bright, multi-coloured rag rugs were everywhere, with a large oval version in front of the fireplace. She had to admit, the place was very homey and nothing like the Spartan boarding school she'd lived at for so many years.

Thinking of school brought a fond reminiscence to mind. With the constant pecking of the nuns, life would have been intolerable if it weren't for her favourite teacher and friend, Miss Imogene Hocking. Imogene would take Kathryn out for lunch or to the theatre or boating on the lake.

If it weren't that Imogene lived in a boarding house and had limited means, Kathryn would not be here in this cobbled-together town now. Instead, she'd be back home, living with Imogene in Toronto, planning how best to acquire the lofty status of *Lady Lawyer*. For, most wonderful of all, Imogene was friends with Miss Clara Brett Martin, a true trailblazer and Kathryn's idol. Miss Martin was the first woman to be admitted as a barrister and solicitor to the Law Society of Upper Canada. In fact, she was the first female lawyer in the whole of the British Empire and Kathryn desperately wanted to be the second.

She dreamed and planned on following in her idol's illustrious footsteps. Clara Brett Martin, this modern-thinking lady, this courageous proponent of women's rights, was a worthy and courageous role model indeed. (Somewhere in the back of Kathryn's mind, she could hear stirring music being played: surely it was a Souza march...) Miss Martin had not given up in the face of overwhelming odds, or let the rantings of some bearded old fellows, smelling of stale tobacco and brandy, prevent her from achieving her dream and Kathryn could do, nay, *would* do, no less. She would look upon this side trip out west as at most, a minor setback, her first hurdle on the road to glorious success.

It was then that she noticed a faded photograph standing proudly on the fireplace mantle. Her attention refocused as she moved closer. Kathryn was surprised to see her father smiling out at her as he stood with his arm casually slung around a girl's shoulders. The girl had to be Aunt Belle. They were both much younger and appeared to be on a picnic. Behind them was a gaggle of strangers. Leaning in, Kathryn peered more closely.

"That's your papa and me at a box social and behind us is your grandmother, Josephte Tourond. The rest are aunts, uncles and cousins you've never met."

Startled, Kathryn jumped, taking an involuntary step back.

Her aunt continued, a note of regret in her voice. "It's a problem that Patrice decided to hide his past. What it means is that we should talk about the way your life will be now. I'll make us a nice cup of tea." She went to the stove and busied herself stoking the firebox, then ladled water from the reservoir into a large black kettle before setting it on one of the lids.

"Who's Patrice?" Kathryn asked, still studying the photo.

"Your father, Katy. He went by *Patrick* when he moved down east, thought it sounded more English...and more white." She jammed another log into the stove. "We'll have tea and then I want to tell you a story."

The light was failing and Kathryn hoped her aunt had more than feeble candles. She spotted several coal-oil lamps placed around the cabin. "Shall I light the lamps?"

"Yes, please, and would you mind putting a match to the wood I've laid? It's going to rain tonight and that means the temperature will fall. It will be chilly."

Kathryn glanced down at her beautiful dress, then at the stone fireplace. "You want me to light the fire? I'm not really attired for it."

Her aunt appraised her niece's fine clothes, then went to one of the kitchen cupboards and opened the door. Hanging on the back was a long pinafore apron which she held out to Kathryn. "That should help. I would suggest you put away that frilly rig and find yourself something more practical."

With a supreme effort, Kathryn held her tongue as she yanked the ugly apron down over her head before stomping to the fireplace. Her aunt was proving somewhat of a trial.

Lighting the kindling soon turned into a challenge. At first, Kathryn stood back and threw lit matches at the wood. This didn't work at all. The matches simply went out. Edging closer, she held the tiny flame to the broken branches, which resulted in smoke and burnt fingers. She decided something more combustible was needed, something that would catch fire immediately.

Eyeing the tidy room, Kathryn spied a newspaper on the table between the chairs. She grabbed it and scanned the date: over a week old. Perfect! Balling it up, she stuffed the newspaper under the wood. Holding a match to the paper, she was rewarded as it caught with a whoosh.

Smiling, she watched the bright flames curl fiery fingers around the twigs which finally gave in and flared to life. By the time her aunt brought the tea, there was a cheery blaze in the hearth and Kathryn felt quite pleased with herself.

"Here we are. Have a seat, Katy." Her aunt set the tray down on the table between the chairs, then turned about as though seeking something. "Did you see my newspaper?"

Kathryn slumped into the chair. Lighting wood was hard work. "Yes, I used it to start the fire."

Her aunt stopped. "You what?"

"The ridiculous kindling wouldn't burn. I needed something that would. The paper was a week old anyway." She fanned her sweaty brow.

Slowly and thoughtfully, her aunt reached out to pour the tea. "I think we should have that talk now as things in River Falls are quite different from what you are used to. First, that paper may have been a week old to some, but it was brand new to me. I acquired it when one of the ladies I sew for was going to throw it out. I know back in Toronto, newspapers are common. Out *here*, they're a special treat."

The way she emphasized the word *here*, made Kathryn wonder what was so special about this shanty town she'd landed in. From what she'd seen, they were truly back-woods and rustic. For goodness sake – these people used *outhouses!*

"Katy, your father was a very good and reasonable man, except he wanted more than he could have at home. While he was growing up, his dream was to become rich, get noticed. The problem was something stopped him, something he had no control over." She picked up her cup. "He was born Métis."

There was that word again. Kathryn raised her chin, rather bravely, she thought. "I don't believe that. My father wasn't like you. His skin was light and his hair blonde, like mine."

Her aunt took a deep breath. "The Métis are a mixed-blood people. We are part Indian and part European. In our family's case, we have French roots which go back to your great-great-grandfather who came to Canada in search of furs. He sold these valuable pelts to the North West Company and then the Hudson's Bay. As time went on, he fell in love with an Indian woman and they married. Their children were the first Métis in our family. What this means is that we can have either Indian or European characteristics or a mix of both. Patrice had French roots, true, but he was only half French; the other half was Cree and that meant many doors were closed to him. He couldn't stand this and so he 'passed' for full-blooded white."

All of this was news to Kathryn, a revelation, one she didn't want to be true. Her former friends at school thought there was something tainted about being of mixed blood. She'd read *Uncle Tom's Cabin*, clandestinely with certain other novels and penny dreadfuls not approved of by the nuns, and she'd heard how the Negroes and mulattos of the United States were treated. It was terrible and that wasn't for her. She liked being white, completely white. And she had enough grief in her life, so much, in fact, that she could be the lead character in a Greek play. In all decency and humanity, her aunt should stop talking this nonsense – but there was a detail unanswered that piqued Kathryn's curiosity.

"Thank you for the history lesson, Aunt Belle, but you haven't explained how the Métis ended up, well, where they are now."

"You mean living in the fringes of society – unwashed and unwanted?" Her aunt's eyebrow rose rather wryly. "After the loss at Batoche, we were branded renegades. The Métis had no choice, my dear. With no place to call home, they were forced to live on the road allowances, the land adjacent to the roads which is owned by the government. Kathryn, we are known as the *Road Allowance People*."

Kathryn felt the earth tilt on its axis. "You're *outcasts!* You live in the ditches? Impossible!" She thought of her life at the private boarding school and of her large home with Mrs. Maples, the cook, and their gardener, Old Sam, who tended the lawns and flower beds. She missed her father terribly and wished with all her heart he were here with her. If only she could fall into a deep sleep to be awakened at some future time when a prince's kiss would save her from all this.

"Sadly, this is true." Her aunt went on. "We have lived on the road allowances for years, and I believe we will continue to live on them for many more. We have families that must be raised and it is preferable to moving around in tents and wagons like gypsies."

Faced with this latest blow, Kathryn was appalled...again. "But I'm not like you. I'm not one of you, you... *Ditch People*." Her voice rose. This wasn't happening to her, it couldn't be. "I'm no vagabond squatter. There must be a mistake."

"No, my dearest. There is no mistake. You will stay with

me and I will do my very best to provide a decent life. I will care for you, as though you were my own daughter." Her lips quivered a tiny bit. "It is all I have to offer, and yet it also everything I have to give."

Kathryn shook her head defiantly. "I won't stay. I don't belong here. I must return to Toronto as soon as possible."

First she'd lost her only living parent, her beloved papa, which was almost too much to bear; then she discovered she was not what she had been raised to believe she was, the daughter of an English mother and a father... Well, now that she thought about it, her papa had been rather vague about his roots. She was a mixed-blood Métis and she had to face the prospect of being one of these Ditch People, these outcasts!

And the tragedies didn't stop at that. There was the envelope she had wrested from Sister Bernadette's hand – Kathryn knew what it contained: a few crumpled bills, her entire inheritance. The lawyers had made sure she wasn't burdened with any debt; unfortunately, there had been virtually nothing left after the dust settled. Life was so unfair. To have all this dropped on her frail and delicate shoulders....

Slumping under the unjust weigh of her misfortunes, she closed her eyes and imagined her future, filled with dirt and despair. If it would do any good, she would have fallen to weeping.

A bright and radiant image of her idol, Clara Brett Martin, shone in her mind.

Clara Brett Martin would not simply sit and let misfortune overtake her, no, she would fight back! Setting her cup down so firmly that it rattled in the pretty flowered saucer, Kathryn cleared her throat. "This is all unacceptable. I want to go home now." She covered her eyes with the back of her hand to dramatically emphasise her point. "This is a nightmare I shan't bear!"

Her aunt sipped her tea and then calmly put down the china cup and stood. "You're tired after your long day. You should sleep and we'll talk more in the morning."

After all her aunt's brutal revelations, the mention of sleep immediately flooded Kathryn with exhaustion. It had been an arduous four-day trip and she'd been on the train since early that morning, not to mention how her bones ached from the savage cart ride and hauling that back breaking trunk. Sleep, deep and numbing, erasing all her cares, would be wonderful.

"My room is up there," her aunt pointed and it was then that Kathryn saw what she had taken for the shadowed ceiling of the kitchen was actually the floor of a small loft. It faced out over the living room and was open except for a log rail across the front edge. Tucked away at the back of the tiny open room, she saw a bed and dresser, a chair and a washstand.

"Then, where do I..."

Kathryn's words trailed off as Aunt Belle motioned across the room, toward a darkened corner near the fireplace. "It's not built yet, but soon you'll have a bedroom of your very own right over here." She stood and moved behind the ornate, high-backed sofa.

Kathryn followed and saw a narrow white iron bedstead in an intricate butterfly pattern, a tiny side table with a lamp and a low chiffonier, all of which she had failed to notice before.

"You can put your things in the dresser and the beautiful bed has a real mattress. Everything's new from the Eaton's catalogue." Her aunt smoothed the patchwork spread. "I made the quilt myself. I hope you like the pattern – double wedding ring, an old favourite of mine."

Kathryn felt her spirits sink even lower. "I'm going to sleep in the middle of the room?"

Aunt Belle's forehead furrowed. "It's hardly the middle of the room, dear, and I've arranged for work to be done. You must realise it's not easy, Katy. My friends, who will help for free and donate the materials needed at no charge, must feed their families first and make a living before they take time from their very long day to build you a private room."

Her aunt's tone was chastising; then she rubbed the back of her neck as though in pain. "I'm sorry. All this must be a shock for you and we're both tired." She shared a small smile. "I'll see what I can do about speeding up your room. Until then, we'll have to make do."

Together they dragged the heavy trunk over near the wall of the imaginary room and while Kathryn sat despondently on the bed, her aunt brought a glass of warm milk before kissing her on the cheek. "Good night, Katydid. I'm very glad you've come to stay."

Kathryn fumed. First Katy and now Katydid! She was being addressed as a stick insect! How could this be happening? She felt like she'd sinned and this was her penance. Sister Bernadette must be laughing all the way back to Toronto!

Her gaze alighted on the steamer trunk. There was no way she would unpack her things. She wasn't going to stay that long. This was not her home and never would be. Somehow she had to find the forty-two dollars to pay her passage back to her old life, her real life.

Setting the glass down on the small bedside table, Kathryn threw open the trunk lid, and lovingly lifted out her most precious possessions – her wonderful books. With great care, she arranged them neatly side by side on the plank floor; their spines aligned like a row of colourful soldiers. She knew a magical secret about books. They could free you from the darkest dungeon. While she was imprisoned here, she would escape into their pages and live in a kingdom of dreams.

There were wondrous stories of knights who slew dragons for fair maidens, and heroes who vanquished monsters to save damsels in distress. These tales of chivalry were Kathryn's favourite and she loved the idea of a brave knight riding in to the rescue. That's what she needed, a white knight who could carry her away from this hovel to a castle with turrets and fancy dress balls and...

But that was only in fairy stories. You couldn't hire a white knight like you could a cook or a gardener.

Kathryn grabbed her nightdress and then remembered that the bathroom was somewhere out there, in the dark. She groaned. "Aunt Belle, I need to use the... lavatory. Where exactly is it?" She could hear the trepidation in her voice, then reasoned that who in their right mind wouldn't be fearful of the unknown horrors that waited in the dark of the outhouse.

Her aunt pointed out the window. "Down the path through the pines. You should take a lantern, Katy. We wouldn't want you falling in, now would we?"

Kathryn peered into the stygian blackness and swallowed. "Impossible!"

Chapter 3

THROUGH THE LOOKING GLASS

The next morning, Kathryn's nose was assaulted by the most delicious smells – fresh biscuits, bacon and... She inhaled deeply. Was that hot maple syrup? And where there was maple syrup, there were pancakes. She positively adored pancakes. Sitting up, she felt disoriented and it took her a second to remember where she was and then, with a terrible rush, she remembered *what* she was.

She was Métis.

She was one of the Road Allowance People, one of the outcasts.

Kathryn flopped back down and pulled the feather quilt over her head, shutting out the light, shutting out the world.

"Katy, time to get up, *ma chère*, breakfast is nearly ready."

Her aunt's voice was annoyingly happy. Kathryn dragged herself out of bed, and, pulling on her coat against the early morning chill, headed for the dreaded pine privy. What was there to be so chipper about?

Washed and dressed in her least pretty skirt and blouse, Kathryn sat at the table and reached for the sturdy teapot.

"Good morning, dear. Did you sleep well?" Her aunt asked, placing a plate on the table. It held two meagre rashers of bacon.

"Umm, yes, I guess so." Kathryn searched for the pancakes.

"That's good, now eat up because we have work to do and you'll need your strength."

She passed Kathryn a basket of strange-looking bread.

"*Li gallette*... bannock... It's like biscuits, Katy, and quite nice with a cup of tea."

Kathryn squinted at a bottle marked *Li Siiroo di Pisaandlii*.

"That's dandelion syrup." Her aunt answered before Kathryn could ask.

"Ah, I thought I smelled maple..." Kathryn prompted.

Her aunt laughed. "Why, yes you did, and of course, we need something to pour the syrup over."

She went to the stove and returned with a plate containing the thinnest pancakes Kathryn had ever seen. They were pitiful. You could practically see through them!

"What kind of pancakes are those?" she asked with a hint of disdain. How sad. This new aunt of hers couldn't even cook pancakes correctly!

"Not pancakes, no, nothing so ordinary. These, Katy," Aunt Belle went on, "are my famous *crêpes du matin* and we have fresh cream and preserves to stuff them with."

Kathryn watched as her aunt took one of the paper-thin

pastries, ladled in wild strawberry jam and a liberal slathering of thick cream, and then rolled the whole thing up into a cornucopia of divine delights. Over this, she sloshed the warm maple syrup.

"Impossible!" Kathryn's mouth watered as she reached for the crepes.

FULL TO BURSTING AFTER WHAT HAD to be the most delicious breakfast of all time, Kathryn was eyeing the fireside chairs for a comfortable haven in which to read, when her aunt stood in front of her brandishing the dreaded apron again.

"You wash up while I prepare the clay."

Kathryn couldn't comprehend the meaning of the out-stretched apron. "Wash up? I washed before coming to breakfast."

Aunt Belle shook the apron. "The dishes, Katydid, the dishes! I'm assuming you know how to clean a kitchen?"

Kathryn felt insulted. "Of course, Aunt Belle. I'm sure a young lady with my education should have no problem with simple domestic duties." She took the apron and surveyed the kitchen. Making crepes with fixings had produced a gigantic mess. The bacon grease had congealed and the plates were a goopy petrified mess. At her home, the cook did the dishes and at school, they ate in the dining hall with a staff that took over when the students were finished. However, she was not about to let Aunt Belle know any of this. She wanted to appear capable and utterly competent, even at this type of drudgery. Pushing up the sleeves on her tasteful white eyelet blouse, she set to work.

The wood stove had a reservoir out of which Kathryn dipped steaming water, pouring it into the dishpan cradled in the dry sink. Adding soap, she scrubbed and rubbed the grimy plates, pots and pans, and then dried the dishes, replacing them in the china cabinet when she discovered they were the only ones in the cabin, and not the Sunday best she'd assumed. When she checked the back of the plates, she was surprised to see they were in fact, quality bone china from a well-known English manufacturer.

After wiping the table and stove, Kathryn lugged the heavy dishpan outside and emptied it onto the road. She polished the table with the beeswax until it gleamed and then swept the floor of every crumb.

By the time she'd finished, she was sweating and her hair had come loose from the stylish chignon she'd fashioned that morning. In truth, she was ready to go back to bed. Instead, she collapsed into one of the wing chairs, sure she'd completely impress her aunt with the speed and skill she'd shown. And as a reward, for the rest of the day, she'd stay curled up in a chair and read her current book. She was at a particularly exciting part where her hero, Sir Giles, whose chivalry was known throughout the pages of her novel, was competing in a joust for his fair maiden's favour.

"Don't feel badly, Katy, with a little more practice, you'll get much faster."

Kathryn sat up with a jolt. Her aunt stood silhouetted in the doorway and her words were like being dowsed with a bucket of cold water. Faster? FASTER!

Impossible! She had practically flown through those nasty chores.

Aunt Belle appraised Kathryn with a critical eye. "You should change into rougher clothes. We wouldn't want to ruin your lovely outfit. Working with clay is dirty work."

It was then that Kathryn remembered the mysterious reference to "getting the clay ready." What clay and why did her aunt have to get it ready? Somehow she didn't think she was going to like whatever was coming next.

"These *are* my rough clothes," she said with apprehension.

"Well then, let me find you something more suitable." Her aunt went to the steep stairs that led to her loft bedroom and scampered up them like a woman half her age, only to return with the ugliest pair of worn denim dungarees and threadbare flannel shirt that Kathryn had ever seen.

She recoiled in horror at the rags. Surely, Aunt Belle didn't expect her to wear them! But her aunt mutely held out the ridiculous outfit, and, as Kathryn accepted it, Sir Giles rode away without her.

"This has to do with the arrangement that made me late to pick you up. The friends I spoke of have offered to help today, and so I jumped at the opportunity. *He who hesitates is lost.*" Aunt Belle marched to Kathryn's makeshift bedroom and pulled the bed from the wall, shoving it against the back of the sofa. At that moment, there was a knock on the cabin door.

"Heavens! They're early. Could you get that, Katy?" Aunt Belle asked as she continued clearing out the sleeping area.

Kathryn didn't know what was coming; what she did know was that there was no way she'd leave her beloved books in harm's way. Hastily retrieving the precious cargo, she carefully stowed the novels in her trunk before going to answer the summons.

She opened the door...and screamed. The head of a deer stared balefully down at her, complete with pointy antlers and a lolling pink tongue!

The deer whirled around and it was then that Kathryn saw it had been slung over the back of a man who would have been given the part of the giant in any fairytale. The formidable visitor had wild black hair accented by a grey streak at the temples and a huge bushy beard that could have used a trim four months ago. He looked very Indian, but remembering Aunt Belle's talk yesterday, she decided he was probably a Métis.

"*Tansi, Mademoiselle*. Belle, she is home?"

"Aunt Belle, there's a deer at the door!" Kathryn called, still mesmerized by the dead animal. "I mean a gentleman wishes to speak with you."

Her aunt, a dirt smudge on her face, came over to join

her niece. "Why, if it isn't Claude Remy, returned from your trap line in the bush. Wherever that hidden camp of yours is, you should think about finding the nearest barber before coming back to civilization."

The big woodsman took no offence. "*Ma* Belle, you are *magnifique*. First ting I do, I bring you a yearling jumper, fresh killed dis morning." A broad grin split the dark beard. "I gut it out back. *Oui?*"

His accent was strange, and Kathryn decided it was sort of French and sort of something else, mixed in.

"*Merci*, Claude. I'll be sure to share the meat with everyone in River Falls. Oh, and we've had a bear through so please, when you're done dressing the buck, don't leave any tasty morsels lying about."

The big man grunted, then walked toward the shed where Nellie was stabled.

Aunt Belle closed the door. "Hmm, I think this venison comes with strings attached, *n'est-ce pas?*" With a shake of her head, she went back to moving Kathryn's belongings.

Kathryn didn't know what her aunt meant by this and before she could ask, another knock sounded through the cabin.

"That will be them and I haven't got the tea made. Katy, would you mind..."

"Curiouser and curiouser." Feeling decidedly like Alice in Wonderland, Kathryn opened the door, wondering what she would find on the other side this time.

The man standing there reminded her of a stork — tall, extremely thin and oddly angular. He had several heavy boards slung over his shoulder and behind him was another fellow, short and stout, carrying a large saw and various other tools.

"Pierre, my favourite carpenter, please *entrez-vous*." Aunt Belle shouted from the kitchen. "I was about to put the tea on."

"*Salut*, Belle. You said your lovely niece needed a room of her own, so we came with our this and our that," Pierre replied. "I brought the *this*," he tapped the planks, "and Joseph brought the *that*." Kathryn swung the door wide, stepping back as the two men tramped in.

"And this beautiful young lady must be Katy, Patrice's girl. Welcome to River Falls, *Mademoiselle*." Pierre paused in front of Kathryn, the boards teetering precariously on his bony shoulder as he touched the brim of an imaginary hat.

"Ah, actually, it's Kathryn," she corrected as he continued past her with the lumber. "And yes, I'm Patrick's daughter. Won't you come in..." she called to his retreating back.

"*Bonjour! Bonjour!*" Pierre's partner Joseph greeted her cheerily as he scurried in, lugging his tools. "*Bonjour! Bonjour!*"

She immediately thought of Tweedle Dee and Tweedle Dum.

Before she could close the door, Kathryn spied a diminutive woman hobbling up the path toward the cabin.

The white-haired matron used a silver-topped black cane carved with the most elaborate decoration and obviously of high quality. Trailing several steps behind was a boy carrying a wrapped bundle. It was her Prairie *Puss-in-Boots*, the same boy she'd seen when they'd arrived in the sliver-infested cart. His large red hat was perched at a jaunty angle and the shiny black feather gleamed in the morning sun.

Kathryn stood at her post of doorkeep, waiting for these newest visitors to arrive. Her aunt had to have the busiest cabin in the west!

The wizened elder stopped at the door and motioned for the lad to give Kathryn the parcel. She took it from him, a tantalizing smell rising from what she hoped was a cake wrapped within.

"*Merci*, JP. Run along now." The grandmotherly woman shooed the lad away with a wave of her cane.

He wiggled his eyebrows impishly at Kathryn, mouth ringed with cake crumbs and icing, no doubt his fee for carrying the delicious package. He was older than she'd first thought; perhaps her age. It was the ridiculous hat that made him seem like a child playing dress-up.

With a wink, he turned and whistling a lively tune, strode back down the path.

"*Mon Dieu!*" The old woman gasped. "That trail gets longer every time I come here." She carefully stepped over the threshold, nodding at the parcel in Kathryn's hands. "This gateau is for the tea I know Belle is making. My name is Madame Ducharme. You may call me Kokum." Her voice was strong and clear.

Kathryn checked the path to see if there were any stragglers, then took the cake inside. She saw the men were already busily constructing two inside walls in the far corner where her room would be and from the framework, it would be a very small room indeed.

The old woman stabbed her cane in their direction. "She will need a proper door. Every young girl needs privacy."

"Francis is bringing one later, Kokum. He'll make sure it's hung before tonight." Joseph answered. "I would have done it myself except Giselle keeps me busy riding all over the countryside for the special herbs and spices she uses in her baking. Some weeks, I'm lucky to make it to Sunday mass." He chuckled. "At the rate they're ordering from us, the ladies of Hopeful will forget how to make a loaf of bread soon."

"And the whitewash? When is that to be done?" the bossy elder demanded of Aunt Belle.

"In its turn, Kokum. The clay and straw are mixed and Katy and I are about to begin. I'll leave the tea to you."

"I need milk. Kathryn, fetch some from the well, girl!"

Kathryn jumped. If the two builders were Tweedle Dee and Tweedle Dum, then this tiny tyrant had to be the Queen of Hearts. All that was needed was the command, *Off with her head!* The Mad Hatter's tea party was already in full swing: dead deer and a crazy woodsman, workers marching around swinging boards and hammers, old ladies who commanded everyone like they owned the place, and now, milk from a well?

Aunt Belle, seeing her confusion, came to her rescue. "We keep dairy goods like milk and butter in the well so they won't spoil. It's cool down there."

"I thought your water came from the river? If you have a well nearby, why not use it?" Kathryn was even more confounded.

"Because the well is nearly dry. There's enough water so it stays damp and that keeps everything cool."

Kathryn started for the door and then stopped. "And this Métis ice-box is where?"

"On the other side of the lean-to. You'll see the pump handle." Her aunt instructed.

Kathryn did as she was bid. Rounding the corner of the shed, she stopped, reeling back at a sight that made her stomach twist. She'd forgotten that Mr. Remy was dressing the deer. From what she could see, it was more like *undressing* the poor creature.

Hurrying past the bloody carnage, she retrieved the milk and raced back to the cabin, ready for a needed rest.

Instead, she'd barely set the quart sealer down when her aunt thrust a bucket mixed with mud and straw at her.

"Enough dawdling, Katy. Time to get started."

Chapter 4

THE THREE LITTLE PIGS, ROBIN HOOD AND THE BIG BAD WOLF

Kathryn took the bucket from her aunt wondering what she was in for next. One peek and her stomach lurched for the second time that day as the dank, fetid smell overwhelmed her.

Glumly, she followed her aunt to the corner of the log cabin where her bedroom was soon to be. "Aunt Belle, what on earth am I supposed to do with this muck?" She held the mud mixture as far from her body as possible.

"This." Her aunt reached into her own bucket with a wooden trowel, scooped out a large gob of the mixture, and then plastered it onto the outer log walls across from the plank ones Tweedle Dee and Dum were busily beavering away at. She did it with so much gusto, you'd have thought she was icing a cake. "We'll put a coat of the straw mix on, filling the chinks and smoothing it over the logs, let it dry, then top coat it with straight clay, again letting it dry so we can fill in any cracks, then finish it off with whitewash. Voila! You'll have a room fit for a queen, or at least a princess, as nice as any back in Toronto. I want you to feel at home."

Gingerly, Kathryn reached into the bucket with a trowel and tried to mimic her aunt's actions. The clay fell off the wall with a disgusting splat.

"Add a little water to keep it sticky," he aunt instructed.

Kathryn poured some water in and tried again. This time the gooey mixture stuck. Trying not to gag, she filled in the spaces between the logs, then scooped out more and spread on a thick layer, making a flat surface, or at least as flat as she could with the uncooperative mud. She felt like she was building one of houses for the Three Little Pigs.

"Good! That's perfect." Her aunt encouraged.

Kathryn's stomach quieted as she figured out the exact consistency needed to prevent the muddy mix from falling off. The work was messy and her arms ached, but she was bound to keep up with her aunt. Before long, she had gobs of muck in her hair, straw chaff on the inside of her shirt and the ugly dungarees were coated in drying clay.

"Wonderful!" her aunt said with satisfaction as she inspected her wall. "Once this is done, we'll let it dry and then put on the smooth coat in a couple of days." She smiled and added, "That one we put on with our hands, Katy."

"You want me to actually touch the vile stuff!" Kathryn sputtered.

"The clay is good for your skin. It pulls out all the impurities, like those fancy mud baths in Europe."

Wincing, Kathryn thought of how the squishy mud would ooze between her fingers and felt nauseous again. The straw mix had the consistency of fresh dog droppings and felt like cold sludge. What must the smooth coat feel like – slippery, slimy?

She swallowed as her stomach told her that it had had enough for one day. But there was no way Kathryn would show discomfort to her aunt and these strangers. She knew the old woman called Kokum had been watching her, judging her. With as much enthusiasm as she could muster, Kathryn went back to applying the clay straw mixture, smearing it over the wall. Now she was grateful that her new room was so small.

As they worked, a succession of Aunt Belle's neighbours stopped by, dropping off various food items. One, Aunt Belle said, was *lii torchiyer*, which Kathryn would have called a meat pie in Ontario; and another dish had the improbable title of *li rababoo di liyev*, which turned out to be rabbit stew. Kathryn's face hurt from the fake smile she kept stitched to her lips as she greeted each visitor politely. She felt like a side show attraction at the circus. Aunt Belle flew through her wall and was soon finished, dropping her trowel into the bucket with a finality that worried Kathryn.

"I'll step over here, out of your way," Kathryn said, backing up so that her aunt could take her place. Their eyes locked for a split second and Kathryn had the sinking feeling that she was being cut adrift on a mud raft in the middle of the ocean. A rogue wave washed over her tiny craft when her aunt rinsed her hands, drying them as she stood in the doorway of the half-built room.

"You're doing fine. I'll sit with Kokum while you finish up."

"Me? But, the logs and the wall and..." She protested, but saw she had no choice. Was this what it was like to be a slave under her master's cruel whip? This was indeed a *Grimm* fairytale. She continued fighting with the clay, listening with one ear to Pierre and Joseph talking while they nailed up the last of the rough-sawn boards.

"I'm telling you, it was him!" Pierre said stubbornly.

"You saw him?" Joseph mumbled, holding several nails in his mouth with his teeth.

"*Oui.*" Pierre assured his workmate. "He was *très formidable* with a black hat and disguised with a mask of silk across his eyes."

The reference to a masked man immediately caught Kathryn's attention and she stopped squishing the mud to eavesdrop more closely.

"It was the *Bandit de Grand Chemin* out doing good works again." Pierre insisted.

Bandit? Black hat? *Mask?* Kathryn forgot about her muddy mess entirely. "What man is this, sir?"

"Why, The *Highwayman,* Miss Katy." Pierre explained eagerly. "He is a true hero. He is the phantom crusader for the Métis of River Falls. When we are cheated, he finds a way to balance the books; when an injustice is done, the Bandit de Grand Chemin rights it."

"What is this cheating and injustice?" Kathryn asked, intrigued.

The two workmen exchanged a glance; then Joseph shrugged. "She will find out soon enough." He hesitated. "The truth is, the town's people, the whites, they don't like us Road Allowance folks. They have their own way of treating the Métis and it's not good. They remind us we are halfbreeds with no rights every chance they get. Sadly, we are often swindled and the law is always on their side. The Highwayman, he takes the problem and corrects things."

Kathryn felt a flutter of excitement. "You mean he robs from the rich and gives to the poor, like, like..." She gasped. "Like Robin Hood!"

Pierre agreed excitedly. "Exactly. He is River Fall's very own Robin Hood."

"This Highwayman, who is he?" Kathryn asked breathlessly, imagining this hero of the underdog.

Joseph shook his head. "No one knows. He is a mystery man."

Kathryn couldn't believe it. Here was a hero who could have stepped out of the pages of one of her books! She had to find out more. A thousand questions jumped up for answers, but when she prompted Pierre and Joseph further, they had none. Her mind raced through stories of merry men and the Sheriff of Nottingham as she finished the loathsome mud coat on the logs.

Finally, the two men nailed up the final board of the two adjoining plank walls, complete with a frame for a door that was yet to materialise. Kathryn swiped on the last of the clay and then stood back to admire her handiwork.

"*Magnifique!*" Pierre exclaimed.

"*Fantastique!*" Joseph agreed.

"Well done!" Aunt Belle added with a laugh, coming to stand beside Kathryn as they all inspected the new walls. "It will look wonderful when we're done."

Kathryn tried to block this thought – more disgusting days of mud and mess ahead of her.

Satisfied, the two men gathered their tools and prepared to leave.

"If we can be of any other help, let us know, Belle." Pierre touched a fingertip to his imaginary hat brim again. "Welcome home, Miss Katy."

And before Kathryn could correct the name or thank them for their help, both men left as unceremoniously as they had arrived.

The only light in her new room was from a small window; still, it was enough that Kathryn could see how nicely her aunt's wall had turned out. By comparison, hers was lumpy and uneven.

"My part's terrible," she moaned dejectedly. Not that she really cared a fig about a mud-smeared wall, but still, she had her pride.

"You've done a splendid job, Katy. It's quite an art form." Aunt Belle tossed Kathryn a wet cloth. "You've earned your cake." Then she hugged her niece as they stood appraising the damp clay walls.

Maybe it wasn't that bad, Kathryn decided, tipping her head a little to the left and trying not to focus on the bigger lumps. After all, she'd never done anything like this in her life before. Yes, in fact, it was not bad at all. When they finally got the smooth clay coat and whitewash on, it would almost be a regular room from a regular house, if you squinted a little. She thought of hanging a lovely picture, maybe one with a castle and a knight on a charger...

Kathryn stopped herself. What was she doing? This was crazy thinking. She wasn't going to stay long enough to worry about such nonsense.

Angrily, she wiped the worst of the grime on the tail of the ugly flannel shirt which hung out of her saggy jeans. She didn't care what these people thought about her appearance. They were about to become history as well.

"I'll stoke up the fires to dry this quickly." Aunt Belle went to the wood box and chose several pieces of birch, then pushed them into the cast iron stove before moving to the fireplace and stirring the ashes until the embers glowed red.

At that moment, there was a perfunctory knock at the door and another man, short and slight of build, arrived carrying a bright green door. He walked in and, without a word, set to work.

"That's Francis. He doesn't talk much; still he's a hard worker." Her aunt whispered quietly as they sat at the table with the old woman.

Kathryn watched the silent man as he expertly and quickly fitted the door. This was especially amazing when she noticed his right hand was frozen with the fingers curled into a claw. "Aunt Belle, what happened to Francis?"

Belle kept her voice down. "He was beaten in town one night and the thugs broke the bones so badly, they never healed right."

Kathryn swallowed. How horrible. She admired the quiet man even more after hearing this.

"You did a decent job, young lady. Soon, you will have a lovely room you can be proud of as you helped to build it." The Queen of Hearts passed Kathryn an extremely thick slice of the cake she'd brought.

"Thank you, Madame Ducharme. You are most gracious." Kathryn decided she may look boorish in her ridiculous peasant clothes, but poor manners simply wouldn't do, even if she did smell like a charwoman.

"I'll remind you to call me Kokum," the elder admonished.

"Yes, ma'am, I mean Kokum." Kathryn amended quickly, feeling as though she were addressing Mother Superior at school.

Kokum poured Belle's tea. "Did you hear Claude Remy is back?"

Belle's lips tightened. "He brought me a lot of fresh meat this morning. I'll be able to make all of us a big pot of *Li Shivreu Pleu Bon.*" Seeing Kathryn's exasperated face, she explained, "My famous Venison Supreme. Very tasty." She turned back to Kokum. "Claude's out back of the shed dressing the deer now."

The old woman nodded as though she understood something unspoken. "He'll be at the dance to welcome Kathryn to River Falls tonight. It's at my place."

"Oh, a dance! That is so kind of you, Rose Marie." Aunt Belle said warmly. "What should we bring?"

The old woman cackled good naturedly, a sound like a raven laughing. "Why, bring yourselves, of course!"

FOR THE DANCE THAT EVENING, Kathryn chose a favourite dress. It was deep rose with ivory lace collar and cuffs, perfectly suitable for any evening's entertainment back home. She spent a long time primping, dabbing her cheeks and lips with rouge from the precious little pot she'd brought with her, a Christmas present from Imogene last year. It had been her first foray into the womanly arts and when she'd shown her father, he'd said she was too young for such a gift, then he'd hugged her, laughing, and told her that try as he might, he couldn't stop time and she was, indeed, growing up. She vowed to keep the tiny jar always.

To complete her ensemble, she added the most precious

thing she owned – a gold locket her father had given her on her fourteenth birthday. She had been thrilled with the extravagance and when she opened it, there were pictures of her parents, one on each side. Her father had said that whatever wonders life brought her way, and no matter what far-flung corners of the world she may visit, their love would be with her always.

Kathryn touched her lips with her fingertips, then, closing her eyes, blew her papa a kiss.

All that remained was to deal with her hair. It was not as thick as she would have liked, and she had to be ever so cautious using the curling tongs. Once, she'd burned a whole swath so badly, the locks had broken completely off when she'd unrolled them. That had been a painful, and embarrassing, lesson. Today, Kathryn was extra careful. She wanted to be flawless so these people could see what a sophisticated young lady she was.

"It's rather later than is socially proper to arrive as a guest, especially the guest of honour, Aunt Belle. We should hurry." Kathryn quickly tied the flounced black wool bolero she was wearing to ward off the night's chill.

Belle laughed. "Don't worry about being late. The party will last till dawn and won't really get going until midnight, when everyone's creaky joints are loosened and the little ones are asleep on the porch."

After hearing this, Kathryn wondered if she was a tad overdressed. It sounded more like an informal family get-together than an evening gala. At last, they set off, talking as they wove their way through the towering pines on the dirt road to Madame Ducharme's.

"You look every inch a proper young lady. Your father would be so proud." Belle smiled at her niece.

"Thank you, Aunt Belle. And I am sure Mr. Remy will be suitably impressed with you."

At this, her aunt's eyebrow twitched as though to comment.

"Your dress..." Kathryn had noticed the precise lines and elegant cut of her aunt's gently worn gown. "... it's perfect."

"Ah, yes. I'm sure Claude still approves of my outfit. It's not the first time he's seen it." Aunt Belle shifted the load she was carrying to her other arm.

They were bringing two hefty baskets of venison to be distributed at the party – an odd hostess gift, to be sure, but after today's experience, Kathryn decided nothing about River Falls' society would surprise her.

Though the moon shimmered silver in the black velvet sky, Kathryn carried a lantern which shone brightly, illuminating the gravel road ahead. As they made their way, Aunt Belle regaled Kathryn with stories of her childhood growing up first in Batoche, then on the Road Allowances. The overall impression was one of a normal family, in fact, more normal than Kathryn's own as she'd spent most of her life at the convent school. Many of the incidents were funny and she couldn't help but laugh at the antics her father had been up to. It was a side of him that she hadn't been aware of.

Suddenly, a horseman sprang from the woods, blocking their path. The horses' hooves stamped and pawed the ground sending swirling dust devils into the air. Panicked, Kathryn held the lantern up as much to see the rider as to let him see her.

The man was in the dark brown field jacket of the North West Mounted Police, the yellow stripe clearly visible on his navy breeches. He pushed his Stetson back on his head.

"What do we have here? Two lovelies out for an evening stroll."

The rider's pale eyes glowed eerily in the moonlight, his teeth a white gash across his face.

"We've no business with you, Constable Blake." Belle spoke calmly as she casually pushed Kathryn behind her.

This was not the reaction one usually had when meeting a member of the police and instantly, Kathryn knew this situation was not good. Surreptitiously, she glanced about, judging the best escape route should it be needed.

"I'm makin' sure no harm comes to you, Belle. This is a mighty lonely stretch of road." The man grinned, and in the lamplight it looked almost like a leer. "Some desperado might rob you of your valuables."

"My *valuables* will stay with me and I pity the man who tries to take them by force." Aunt Belle drew herself up and raised her chin defiantly.

There was something going on here that Kathryn couldn't understand and it had nothing to do with the baskets of venison. The man appeared odd for some reason, but Kathryn couldn't put her finger on it. She shifted the lantern, and, with a jolt, saw what it was.

He had no ear on the right side of his head! A mutilated flap of angry red skin, twisted and torn, hugged his skull where his ear should have been. She recoiled, shuddering.

Much to Kathryn's surprise, instead of backing away from the intruder as she had, Aunt Belle stepped boldly forward, causing the skittish horse to shy.

The constable reined his mount in with a vicious yank on the bit. "What's your hurry? Got some eager buck waiting?" His attention then shifted to Kathryn. "And who's this? Dang, you are a sweet little thing. I ain't seen you with these squatters before and you sure don't look half breed with that pretty yellow hair an' all."

The grin was definitely a leer now, and Kathryn's throat went dry. "My name is Kathryn Tourond and I'm visiting my aunt," she whispered, unable to force any more air out of her lungs.

Blake leaned over his saddle and rested his arm on the pommel, appraising her. "In that fancy dress, you're like a present waitin' to be unwrapped." He spit tobacco juice into the dust. "Suits me fine."

Kathryn's skin crawled.

"I've no time for this nonsense, Cyrus." Belle's voice rang with steely determination as she reached back for Kathryn's arm. Holding the basket in front of her like a shield, she pushed passed the horse and moved quickly down the road.

Kathryn's heart was beating so loudly, she was sure her aunt could hear it.

"Don't pay that village idiot any mind. Cyrus Blake's one of the Mounted Police here to bring order to the lawless territories." Her tone said this was not necessarily the case. "He's not like any Mountie I've ever met. I don't know how Sergeant Prentiss – he's the constable's boss – stands the lazy lout. Many brave young Canadian men are fighting for the Empire against the Boers in Africa and from what I've heard, Blake only joined the North West Mounted Police to avoid enlisting. Tells you a little about his character, or lack of it. One thing's for certain, that man's got a mouth on him. The best way to deal with his sort is to stay out of his way."

Kathryn had the utmost respect for the North West Mounted Police, especially when they were in their scarlet dress uniforms, so polished and splendid, like handsome knights of old riding around on their chargers maintaining the right. This Constable Blake, however, must have failed his class in chivalry.

She sighed. It was always the same, never a white knight around when you needed one. Preferably one with a huge battleaxe and a razor-sharp sword, maybe a mace or two with extra long spikes.... She'd never admit it, but this incident had truly frightened her. She's been so scared, she could hardly speak.

On the other hand, her aunt had been amazing. She slid a sidelong peek at Aunt Belle and could detect no trace of fear on the strong woman's face. Impossible!

Chapter 5

ROBIN HOOD IN ALBERTA AND A TRUE BLACK KNIGHT

The scene Kathryn and her aunt arrived to at Madame Ducharme's was very strange. Lights blazed from every window of the tumbledown shack; the staccato notes of a violin playing a fast tune rang out and it appeared that all the furniture had been removed from the house and piled haphazardly on the grass! They threaded their way past a settee and breakfront, then chairs and a wire birdcage hanging from a tall stand. When Kathryn peeked under the cloth covering the cage, she found herself nose to beak with a large, black and white magpie! What kind of crazy place was this?

"I can hear that Monsieur Arcand has brought his best fiddle tonight." Belle laughed, the earlier incident with the constable seemingly forgotten. "He can play from dusk till dawn with only water to keep him going."

When they entered the small house, Kathryn was amazed. The place was filled with noise as children ran about yelling, chasing each other and any unsuspecting dog or cat that didn't escape fast enough. Adults clustered against the walls, laughing and talking over the lively music and stamp of feet, and in the centre, dancers were weaving and turning. No wonder the furniture had been removed.

Passing their baskets to one of the welcoming ladies who were preparing the food, Kathryn noted that all the men wore brightly coloured woven belts. "Why are they wearing those red scarves around their waists?"

Aunt Belle lifted her gaze heavenward. "Oh, Patrice, if you were here, I'd box your ears. Katy, those are *lii soncheur flesheys*."

Like the other phrases she'd been hearing here in River Falls, it sounded French, but not like the French she'd learned in convent school. Still, Kathryn gave it a try. "*Les ceintures flêchés...* ?"

"They're Red River sashes, my dear, and we Métis wear them to show our history and pride, much like a Scotsman wears his tartan kilt."

Nudging their way through the throng, Aunt Belle led her to the scattering of chairs lining the wall and on which were sitting the old people of the community, including Madame Ducharme.

"How is our girl's room coming along?" the grandmotherly lady demanded before either Aunt Belle or Kathryn had a chance to sit.

"*Tres bien!*" Aunt Belle assured her with a good natured laugh. "Tomorrow, the smooth clay, then two coats of whitewash and it will be perfect. Once that's done, Katy can move her belongings in and unpack her trunk."

Kathryn didn't say a word at this. She had no intention of unpacking anything. She needed a plan to earn the train fare back to her real life and then, like the clever damsels being held prisoner in her stories, she would find a way to escape.

A gentleman walked up to Aunt Belle and spoke rapidly, her aunt replying in the same strange tongue. Again, it sounded like French – but only sometimes. Kathryn didn't understand a word.

"What language was that?" Kathryn asked when the man walked away.

"Hmm, I'm guessing this is another omission on my brother's part. That's Michif, the Métis language. It's part French and part Cree," her aunt explained.

"Much like us!" Kokum cackled in that odd way she had.

"Well, it's quite rude to speak a foreign tongue in front of those who can't understand." Kathryn felt insulted, and a little left out. She suspected that they had been talking about her.

Kokum looked thoughtful and then the old woman stamped her cane on the floor to get everyone's attention. "In honour of our newest community member, we will speak only *Anglais* so that she can join in with her new neighbours."

The crowd murmured agreement and those who had

been speaking Michif immediately switched to English. Kathryn felt her face flush at the furor she'd caused; however, it made things much easier when well-wishers stopped to welcome her.

"Belle, *ma chère*, come now. John, he plays da Red River Jig next."

At the interruption, her aunt stopped talking to Kokum and they all looked up.

Claude Remy's appearance was much improved since Kathryn had seen him that morning. The man-mountain had trimmed his beard and slicked back his hair with some kind of grease that shone in the lamplight.

Kathryn sniffed, then whipped out her handkerchief and held the scented lace to her nose. What on earth was that reek?

She coughed politely to cover her reaction, hoping no one noticed, then sniffed again. Mr. Remy – actually, his *coat* – smelled horrible!

The trapper wore a buckskin jacket emblazoned with an ornate and quite stunning flower beadwork pattern. Memorable as this may be, it was the overpowering odour wafting toward her that Kathryn would remember most. Her eyes were practically watering.

"I'm talking to Rose Marie right now, Claude," Aunt Belle said in a controlled voice. "I'll be with you in a moment." She went back to her conversation with the elder.

The big man stepped closer. *"Non!* Dis is dat favourite

fiddle music of mine."

Belle straightened her spine stiffly, a gesture Kathryn had made herself many times in the past. Claude took a step back.

Before Belle could say a word, the scene was interrupted by a young man wearing a bright red hat with a feather tucked in the side. It was the Prairie Puss-in-Boots.

"Care to dance, Mademoiselle?" he asked in a soft voice as he doffed the flamboyant fedora.

Kathryn waited to see what her aunt would do in the face of this latest bid for her attention.

Her aunt had an unmistakable twinkle of mischief in her eye. "Well, Katy? Do you want to dance?"

"Me?" Kathryn was taken aback at the unexpected invitation. "Dance? Lord, no! Ah, I mean, no, thank you."

"Another time, then." The boy bowed politely and melted back into the crowd. Flustered, Kathryn knew she'd been rather rude to the young man. How could she explain she'd refused simply because she didn't know how to do this wild, outrageous dancing? There were not a lot of dances back at the Academy for Young Ladies, and even when there were, her dance card had never been what you would call full.

Kokum waved dismissively. "There's all night to talk. Belle, you are twenty-six now, people will gossip if they don't see you dancing. They say it's time for you to move on and let the dead rest." A weak smile struggled at the corners of her mouth. "Why don't you show our Kathryn how a toe tappin' jig should be done so she'll know for the next time a young man asks her to join him."

The flash of impatience that crossed her aunt's face was noticed only by Kathryn as Aunt Belle laid her shawl aside and moved gracefully to the centre of the floor with Claude.

It was then Kathryn saw her aunt also had one of the red sashes draped from her shoulder and tied off at the waist. She and her partner slipped effortlessly into the intricate dance, keeping perfect time to the music. The crowd cheered when the fiddler picked up the tempo; the ladies skirts flared and the men's sashes flew. Kathryn marvelled at what she was later told was the Reel of Eight and then the Broom Dance, which was performed with an actual broom. She thought that one most ingenious.

As the excitement rose, Kathryn found herself clapping along with the other bystanders. This was like nothing she'd seen back in Toronto and, truth be told, she was enjoying it immensely. It was as though everyone in the house belonged to one huge family. The main object of the dance seemed to be simply to have fun and laugh. Here you were allowed to stamp and clap, holler and whistle, which was an inexcusable breach of etiquette back home.

As Kathryn watched Aunt Belle being whirled around the floor, she thought of the old woman's words and wondered if there had been a tragic romance in her aunt's past.

"Kokum, you said that Aunt Belle should 'let the dead

rest.' Did someone close to her pass away?"

The elder lowered her head. *"Oui, c'est tellement triste.* Poor Claude has been pursuing our Belle for a long while now, but Belle was in love with my son, Gabriel, and turned him down. Belle and Gabe, so much love..." Her eyes grew misty. "They were to be married, then sadly there was some bad business and my boy had to run or be lynched."

This shocked Kathryn. She'd heard of lynching Negroes in the United States, but surely there was never anything so terrible in Canada. "Was it vigilantes?" she asked breathlessly.

Kokum hesitated, weighing her words, as though to judge whether this young girl would be allowed to know something very dark indeed. Kathryn sat up ramrod straight, her hand gently pressed to the side of her cheek, trying for an air of composed maturity. She wished she'd brought long gloves, preferably ivory lace, to help with the overall effect. Her attempt at a mature demeanour appeared to satisfy Kokum as she cleared her throat and continued with the story.

"It was a little over a year ago it happened. That despicable Constable Cyrus Blake stopped a young River Falls girl walking home alone after a dance one night."

Caught off guard at hearing the man's name again so soon, Kathryn inhaled sharply. "We had a run-in with him on the road this evening. I was so..." She was going to say terrified, then thought that made her sound like a frightened little girl, afraid of the bogey man. "*Startled* when he came across us on that deserted road. Fortunately, Aunt Belle resolved things nicely."

Kokum's head bobbed knowingly. "I bet she did. Belle's no coward; she's no fool either. She knows how hard to push and when." She twisted her ancient gold wedding band. "Now, where was I? Oh yes. What happened that night was terrible. That animal Blake, he was... *hurting* our little girl when Gabriel showed up and fought him off. The constable pulled a knife and they wrestled. Somehow, the knife got turned around and Blake sliced off his own ear! Gabriel knew he would be killed for this. He had no choice, so my son ran. The constable vowed to get revenge; wanted to string Gabe up and let the vultures have him. Somehow, Blake found out my son was hiding in Medicine Hat. He tracked Gabe down and shot him in the back. Belle can't get past Gabriel's death and remains a spinster."

"How terrible," Kathryn whispered reverently. Constable Blake was the very definition of a Black Knight with a heart of pure evil.

Despite the undeniable tragedy of the tale, she felt an inexplicable thrill. This was like something she would read in a dime novel. How *tragique*. How exciting. How wild-west!

Then she saw the devastating grief etched on the face of the old woman and immediately, Kathryn felt remorse and wished she hadn't brought it up. She quickly changed subjects. "I heard Aunt Belle call you Rose Marie, but you have asked me to call you Kokum. Is Kokum also your name?"

"No, no, girl!" The elder spoke as though Kathryn was being silly – again. "Kokum is grandmother in Cree. You are to live with us, and will naturally be one of my honorary grandchildren." She made a contented sound. "As is everyone in River Falls. Much easier that way – I don't have to remember who is and isn't related and if you ever need a grandmother, *voilà*, I am always available."

There was something about this that touched Kathryn. She resisted the feeling. She wasn't going to live here for long and she had no grandmother. She wanted her old life back, with her father alive and her studies at the convent school and walking along the paved streets with Miss Hocking, and, and... A powerful wave of homesickness hit her. She desperately wanted to be back in Toronto where she belonged.

The truth was, she couldn't bear the thought of a life here, with these primitive conditions and backward ways. Today's mud-wall torture gave her a glimpse of what lay ahead. In fact, the only thing that had interested her at all since she'd arrived had been the conversation with Pierre and Joseph about the Highwayman. Now, that was something.

Kathryn focused on the soft lantern light, letting her mind flow out to that man in Lincoln green, the pheasant feather in his jaunty hat swaying as he leapt from log to rock, deftly escaping the dastardly Sheriff of Nottingham who hunted him so relentlessly. She saw sturdy Little John and stout Friar Tuck, and, waiting for her hero to rescue her, beautiful and brave Maid Marian, dressed in a lovely dark rose dress with ivory lace collar and cuffs....

"Katy.... Katy...."

Kathryn blinked, then looked into the face of her aunt. Claude Remy stood close behind, preening as though he'd won the blue ribbon for the best heifer at the fair.

"I thought you two ladies needed some refreshments." Belle set down a tray on which perched three cups of tea.

"Oh..., why thank you. The dancing was," Kathryn hunted for the words to describe it. "spirited and," she had to be honest, especially with herself, "quite wonderful."

Belle laughed. "That wasn't dancing, that was good old fashioned jigging, and darn fine jigging at that. Whew!" She puffed out her breath, blowing an errant strand of hair off her dewy face.

Claude shook his head. "Dat white man, he don't know what he miss when he not Métis." His laughter, deep and rumbling, was like thunder. "One day, God, he put dem all in dey's place for how dey treats our people, especially that *cochon* Blake."

The giant man spit noisily which offended Kathryn, and then she saw the spittoon tucked against the wall. He'd hit it dead centre. It was easy to read the hate on Claude's face and there was something else too, something she couldn't put her finger on. Kathryn suspected there was history between the creepy constable and Mr. Remy.

"Now, now, Claude. Let's leave that talk outside." Kokum admonished the big trapper. "Tonight, we welcome this young lady."

He turned back to Belle. "Come, *ma chère*, we do some more jiggin' now dat the fiddle she's warmed up."

Claude reached out to take Belle's arm. In a deceptively quick sidestep, she avoided the grab and moved away. "I must be polite, Claude, and stay with my niece and Kokum. Please feel free to enjoy the party without me." She motioned to a line of young women who had congregated near the far wall.

Mr. Remy's countenance grew dark. He grunted something in Michif, then turned and swaggered over to the giggling mademoiselles.

"I think I'm getting too old for this nonsense," Belle said, fussing with her skirt as she sat. "I'll be glad when I can stop."

Kathryn thought this an odd comment as her aunt had been excited to come to the dance. Perhaps their encounter with Constable Blake had bothered her more than she'd let on. No matter – right now, Kathryn had other things on her mind.

"Aunt Belle, I heard the most extraordinary bit of news today," she said excitedly. "There's this mysterious fellow called the Highwayman, and he's like Robin Hood, he steals from the rich and gives to the poor. Have you heard of him? What can you tell me about this masked man?"

At first Aunt Belle appeared taken aback at the abrupt

change of subject, then she pursed her lips in a gesture so similar to one Kathryn's father used to make that, for a second, a lump closed Kathryn's throat.

"My, you are inquisitive!" her aunt exclaimed. "Yes, the Highwayman is somewhat of a folk hero around these parts. Some months back, there were several incidents that left our neighbours cheated and this stranger stepped in to settle things more fairly. Sadly, this is part of the life on the road allowances; there is no real justice and we must hope for the best when dealing with, well, anyone who is not Métis."

"Why don't the North West Mounted Police make sure everything is fair for the Ditch People?" Her aunt scowled at this label and Kathryn winced. It had slipped out before she'd had a chance to censor herself.

"Katy, the North West Mounted Police don't interfere in business affairs – and anyway, it would come down to their word against ours. And in cases like this, it always ends up with the whites in the right."

Kathryn thought this terrible. "They should vote in a law to ensure justice is done."

"Except we don't get to vote, *ma chère.*" Her aunt took a sip of her tea.

"Yes, yes, because you're a woman and women aren't allowed. I'm talking about the men." Kathryn knew her father had voted.

"No, Katy." Her aunt spoke as though Kathryn had reverted to that very young child again. "None of the Road

Allowance people can vote. We don't own the land we are on and so we don't pay taxes which means we are not allowed. It also means we can be driven off at any minute, as has happened so many times."

"What do you mean?" Kathryn asked.

"This is government land and if the municipality wants to use it for roads or some farmer needs a new pasture and strikes a convenient deal with the local officials, we must leave and after we're gone, the good citizens burn our homes so we cannot return."

Kathryn was stunned. She thought of Aunt Belle's cozy little house reduced to a pile of cold, black ashes. Where would her aunt live? What a terrible predicament to be in – powerless and at the mercy of people who had already cheated and swindled you and who would rather you disappeared. No wonder the families of River Falls helped one another; no wonder they enjoyed themselves so intensely at evenings like this one. Who knew when it could all go up in a fiery blaze?

And where was the law in all this? She could easily see the need for the Highwayman, the Métis Robin Hood. There was only one word Kathryn could think of to express her outrage. *"Impossible!"*

LATER THAT NIGHT, as they strolled home through the sweet-smelling pines, Kathryn's thoughts continued to swirl around the Highwayman. Who could he be – and was he handsome? Surely he was; and young, and passionate.... "Do you know any other stories about the Highwayman? Has he ever rescued anyone from a tower in a lonely castle?" she asked dreamily.

Her aunt smiled at this. "We don't have a lot of castles around here; still, I know some who owe him a debt of thanks. The gentleman who helped build your room, Pierre, he was the first to benefit from the *Bandit de Grand Chemin*. Pierre painted the outside of the hardware store for the owner, Mr. Campbell. He bought the paint and did the work and then, when he went to collect payment, Mr. Campbell said he wasn't happy with the job and refused to pay. Pierre was out the cost of the paint and four days' worth of hard work and could do nothing about it. A week later, he woke to find three gallons of paint sitting on his step, along with two bags of oats which covered the cost of his labour." She laughed softly. "Everyone said it was only a coincidence that the very same hardware store he'd painted had been broken into and certain items gone missing."

"And it was the work of the Highwayman?"

Aunt Belle was noncommittal. "Perhaps. No one knows for sure..."

Even in the dim light of the lantern, Kathryn could see that telltale twinkle in her aunt's eye.

"Another time concerns Henri Beauchamp. He doesn't live here; instead, he's way down by the big bend in the

Old Man River. He has this amazing red hair—it sticks out from his head like a fiery haystack. Anyway, he needed money so he sold his last hog to a white man who then ran Henri off with a gun – without paying for the hog." She picked up a stone from the path, examined it, and then, finding it wanting, tossed it spinning into the woods. "Now you have to understand, Henri Beauchamp is a proud man and stubborn to boot. He told no one how tough things were, never complained, simply kept on trying to make a living for his family. After the animal was butchered, two large hams mysteriously disappeared from the white man's smokehouse and reappeared at the Beauchamp farm which was a very good thing as the family had been reduced to eating gophers."

"*Gophers!* You can't be serious! You mean the little rodents that run around in the dirt?" To Kathryn, this was abominable.

"When your children are starving, Katydid, meat is meat."

"And this was the Highwayman again?"

"Or God balancing the scales. One thing we know for sure is that if they could catch him, the law would put our Robin Hood in jail and throw away the key."

Kathryn would love to meet this hero, whoever he might be.

They walked on in the still evening, but when they reached the place in the path where Blake had accosted them, Kathryn involuntarily shuddered. She peered into the dark forest but could see nothing. "Maybe we should have asked Mr. Remy to escort us home."

"We'll be fine," her aunt assured her, but she moved a little closer to Kathryn.

It was such a protective gesture, unexpected and very welcome that Kathryn immediately felt better. "I want to thank you for taking me to the dance tonight. I truly enjoyed myself."

"I'm glad you liked it because, as you will find out, we have a lot of get-togethers here in River Falls. I think we will have to work on your jigging for the next dance." Aunt Belle did a complicated step in the dust, too fast for Kathryn to catch.

"Mr. Remy, he sure likes to jig up a storm."

"*Oui*, but he is a little, shall we say, too insistent?" Belle laughed at this.

"He certainly didn't take no for an answer," Kathryn agreed. She'd noticed the big woodsman was also very possessive and obviously still had feelings for Belle.

Her aunt hadn't been too forthcoming when it came to admitting any romance between them – maybe it was her way of being coy or keeping it discreet. Whatever the reason, this had been Kathryn's cue, as mysteries were her weakness.

"Mr. Remy was so adamant in squiring you about this evening..." She kept her tone light and innocent. "I'm surprised he didn't *insist* on escorting you home."

Belle pulled her shawl a little tighter around her shoulders. "Actually, Claude did wish to walk me home. He lost some enthusiasm when I said it would be *us* he escorted. I assured him he should stay at the party and it didn't take too much persuading to convince him."

"I'm assuming he could come and go from the party so he could have walked *us* home, sat with *you* on the porch swing and then *he* could have returned?'

"Oh, yes. People often leave and come back. I felt that after our busy day, I'd rather go home without any complications."

Kathryn thought *complications* was an odd way of referring to a suitor. There was something else she wanted to ask her aunt which would require some diplomacy as she didn't want to be offensive. "About Mr. Remy," she wrinkled her nose at the memory, "he certainly was courtly tonight, all cleaned up and his hair so shiny." She paused. "And that unusual coat of his with the beautiful beadwork..."

About then, she noticed her aunt's lips had curved into the shadow of a smile. "Oh yes, we Métis are famous for that flower design. In fact, we're known as the Flower Beadwork People." The smile grew a tiny bit.

"Well, I was wondering, that coat, it sort of, well, it..."

"Had a rather strange bouquet?" Her aunt's restraint evaporated as she choked back a girlish giggle.

"Actually, it was a little...pungent." Kathryn agreed tactfully.

"That's because it was brain tanned and smoked. Surely, they taught you about brain tanning at that fancy school of yours?"

"I must have missed that class." Kathryn made a face, her own laughter bubbling up.

"After the kill, the brain is dug out of the animal's skull and when boiled, enzymes ooze out. The hide is stuffed into the pot with the brain and the chemicals tan it, preventing rot."

Kathryn couldn't believe she'd heard correctly.

Her aunt continued the lesson. "Oh, it's a very useful way to preserve the hides. There are lots of tricks to tanning hide. For instance, to remove the hairs, one needs a mild acid: in the old days, urine was used and for some processes, you rub dog dung into the hide. There's also a smoking step, so it remains soft if it gets wet. That really adds a distinctive note, which you noticed."

Kathryn was aghast...smushed brains, urine, dung, smelly smoke. Her aunt was a font of information, way too much information, in fact.

"The next time Claude is tanning, you should go and see. It's unforgettable. He might even let you scrape off the bits of flesh and fat, which is the first step."

This was the limit for Kathryn. "It sounds very...*educational*, and messy...followed closely by disgusting."

Her aunt laughed and Kathryn joined her. The very idea of it. Impossible!

Chapter 6

IN NEED OF A POISONED APPLE

The next morning was glorious – sunny and warm. Kathryn and her aunt were up early, applying the smooth coat of clay to Kathryn's room. They chatted about the dance, the people of River Falls, then fell into a companionable silence.

Again, Kathryn was very slow, while her aunt swooshed through her wall in record time. Then something surprising happened. Aunt Belle, instead of leaving Kathryn to slog on alone as she'd done with the straw mix, blithely and without a word set to work on the unfinished half of Kathryn's wall.

"With this heat, we'll be able to do the whitewashing later today; then you can officially move in. You'll have a lovely room, Katydid."

Kathryn didn't say a word as her aunt picked up the clay buckets and took them outside.

Since her aunt was dealing with the bucket mess, Kathryn decided she would make tea and re-heat some bannock. After much poking and stoking, she got the fire going and had made tea by the time her aunt, who had gone to her tiny room to change, came down the ladder cradling a bundle in her arms.

"I finished these early this morning." Aunt Belle set the pile of neatly folded dresses on the end of the table and sat for her tea. "Mrs. Prentice, she's the Sergeant's wife, wants them delivered today. It should take about twenty minutes to make it to the barracks."

This puzzled Kathryn. Twenty minutes might take them to the train station, which was halfway to Hopeful – but she didn't recall an army encampment there. "Are you talking about going to Hopeful?"

"Yes, of course, Katy. To the North West Mounted Police detachment office. Locals call it 'the barracks'." Her aunt explained.

"One of the ladies at the dance mentioned it was miles to town and would take an hour with a wagon."

Her aunt had a devilish look in her eye. "The distance remains the same, but with a good horse and better buggy, I can shorten the time."

This made no sense – but Kathryn was beginning to get used to her aunt talking in riddles. Running her fingertips over the soft material of the finely stitched dresses, she noted the superior craftsmanship. "This is how you make your living, you mend clothes?"

"Actually, I do more than mending. I design and tailor ladies dresses and I also do millinery work in a pinch. These are my creations."

"You made these? They're exquisite!" Kathryn was amazed at the intricate detailing on the bodices. She held up one of the dresses – carefully keeping it from her own muddy clothes – to inspect it more closely. "It's flawless." She set the frock back down on the table. "I can't sew at all. The nuns tried to teach me, and discovered I have two left thumbs." Kathryn wiggled her fingers to emphasize the point. "I think I'll spend the day catching up on my reading." Sir Giles was about to joust for his fair lady as unbeknownst to him, that cad, Sir Robert of Worsley, has rigged the contest with faulty lances! Kathryn could hardly wait to find out what happened next.

Aunt Belle pursed her lips. "Hmm, speaking of reading, that brings up a point. You need to continue with your studies. Do you have any school books with you?"

Kathryn had no intention of going to school anywhere except Toronto, and the next term didn't start until September. By the time autumn rolled around, she'd be gone from River Falls. She was sure the good Sisters, with their hearts of soft gold, would take her back, and she'd worry about the tuition when that detail came up. Would it matter to them that she was Métis? Unfortunately, Sister Bernadette was a known blabbermouth, so she was sure this bit of tittle tattle was well known. Otherwise, she could pass like her father....

Kathryn thought about living that lie. Her whole life a fabrication – she couldn't do it. Maybe she wasn't as strong as her father. Besides, how could she become a lawyer like the indomitable Clara Brett Martin if the first thing she did was lie about her heritage?

"It's too late in the year to enrol here. I'll wait until the fall and we can discuss it then." Kathryn didn't actually care about what she was sure were inferior schools out here in this wasteland; still, she was a little curious. "What grades are offered at the River Falls School?"

"None, dear." Aunt Belle shook her head. "We have no proper school. I was talking about home schooling."

Kathryn raised an eyebrow. "Home schooling?" She wasn't sure what form of academia was required to become a lawyer, but she was positive that sitting in a kitchen chair reviewing the multiplication tables would not be part of her scholarly studies! "Completely inadequate!"

"Well, that's how we manage here." Her aunt busied herself refolding the dress.

"Surely there's a school in Hopeful?" Kathryn asked.

"Oh, yes. The Carter Academy; and from what I hear, it's a fine one, quite fancy, with teachers boasting many qualifications and certificates." Her aunt poured them both more tea. "Unfortunately, Katy, you have to put that out of your head. That's not for us."

The tone in her voice alerted Kathryn. "What do you mean, *not for us?*"

"Us, *us* – the Road Allowance People! We can't go to a white school, dear." She retrieved the plate of bannock from the oven and gave each of them a generous piece along with a dollop of rich, yellow butter.

Kathryn gaped at her aunt, hearing the words, and yet rejecting the meaning. It was crazy; it was ridiculous; it made her angry. "You're saying I couldn't go to school because of the colour of my skin!"

Her aunt glanced at her. "Well, not the actual colour dear, you're as peaches-and-cream as they come...No, you wouldn't be allowed because your father was Métis."

This again! Kathryn was beginning to develop a new respect for her father. Despite his precarious position, passing for white in the world, he had always had a wide tolerance for all people. He had remembered that he was himself an outcast because of something he had no control over.

This was 1901, a new century with a new king, new ideas and possibilities and surely, new enlightenment. Not that she would attend, but what if some other child of River Falls wanted a life that was more than living on gophers and doing odd jobs? To be denied, well, *anything* because of one's race. Impossible!

Aunt Belle's sigh shouted resignation even though her voice was a whisper. "You can't fight this, Katydid. Believe me, I've tried. It's the way of the world, our world here in River Falls at least. I know our best hope for freedom is through education. It's the key to giving our youngsters a brighter future – which is why we do the best we can with home schooling." Belle pushed her plate of untouched bannock away.

Kathryn hated injustice. It positively cried out to be remedied and she, Kathryn Marie Tourond, had heard that cry and would take up the torch. She stood, shoving the chair back with a little too much energy. "I shall go clean up, then accompany you to town and we shall see about this school."

With imagined pennants snapping in the breeze, Kathryn marched to the stove for the hot water she'd need to scour off her own coating of clay which had hardened to something resembling granite. She felt like a noble knight, cleansing his body and soul before riding into battle.

SCRUBBED AND SHINING with righteous fervour, Kathryn stepped outside onto the veranda, and stopped abruptly. "This is your *usual transportation?*"

Her aunt was sitting atop the most amazing contraption in the world. Unlike the heavy Red River cart, this sleek little four-wheeled carriage was lightly built, brightly painted, and looked agile and fun. Kathryn was enthralled at first sight. This must have been how Cinderella felt when she saw her golden coach.

Seeing the look on Kathryn's face, Aunt Belle smiled conspiratorially. "I see you like her. This little green beauty is a Spider Phaeton and she's fast. We'll make it to Hopeful in no time."

Of this, Kathryn had no doubt.

Nellie was already hitched up and Aunt Belle was closing a narrow storage box fitted behind the passenger bench. "That's the dresses all packed away. You ready to go?"

Her aunt had taken the precaution of fastening a long leather belt complete with buckle across the seat which she said would hold them in should they hit a hole or rock. Once they set off, Kathryn was very glad for the safety strap.

The ride was wild! They flew down the road, the horse forgetting it was ready for the glue factory, and instead, speeding the small carriage at amazing velocity through the countryside.

Several times, they came upon other horses, buggies or wagons, which quickly pulled out of the way when they saw who was barrelling down on them at that lightning pace. Her aunt would wave and call greetings that were swept away on the wind as they sped past.

It was outrageous behaviour; completely unlady-like...and Kathryn loved it!

When they arrived at the Mounted Police detachment, in an impossibly short span of time, Kathryn was breathless, her hair hanging down from its pins and her clothing in disarray.

"She's something, isn't she?" Aunt Belle's face glowed.

Kathryn was unwilling to admit how exhilarating the ride had been.

"Someday there will be laws governing the speed at

which you can travel down a public road, Aunt Belle, and you shall have to reign in your penchant for foolhardy driving." Kathryn was the tiniest bit disturbed at how much her words sounded like they'd come straight from Sister Bernadette's reproving repertoire.

"Well, until they do, we're in for some high times, Katydid!"

Unfastening the safety belt that had held them secure in the careening buggy, her aunt jumped down, then retrieved the dresses from the seat box and took them into the log building marked simply 'N.W.M.P.'.

Giving her surroundings a critical and judgmental eye, Kathryn decided Hopeful wasn't exactly a bustling metropolis. Perhaps a better moniker for this backwater whistle-stop would have been *Hopeless,* considering the packed dirt streets and hitching posts she saw. And from the ample evidence left on the dusty thoroughfare, she could see the hitching posts were a necessity.

On the other hand, it did seem to be quite a mercantile centre if the number of stores lining both sides of the street was any indication. As she watched, a man in a dingy brown uniform crossed the road and came in her direction. Kathryn's pulse sped up. He was tough and rank, mean and nasty and very familiar. She held her breath. It was Constable Blake.

As he passed, she noticed again the mutilated stub of an ear on the side of his head. Kokum's words came back to her. This man had shot Gabriel Ducharme down in cold blood. In Toronto, that would make him a murderer; here he was a respected member of the North West Mounted Police. In the dark, Kathryn had not noticed his shabby uniform, nor how in need of repair it was. One of the brass buttons was missing and the left pocket had torn, then been badly stitched together.

Wanting to avoid any further contact, she studiously inspected her fingernails, noting the need for a manicure. Blake continued past her and into the detachment office.

Studying the street, Kathryn noticed as another man, young and tall, strode down the wooden boardwalk swaggering a little, which added an air of confidence. He was dressed rather smartly in a checked shirt and gabardine trousers. There was something about him that was undeniably attractive and, best of all, he was coming straight toward her!

Mindful of the frantic ride, Kathryn hastily pinned her hair back into a semblance of tidiness and straightened her clothes. As they were going to the Carter Academy, she'd chosen her attire with care. She wore a tailored black bombazine skirt with a fitted blouse in a lovely sage green. The blouse had a stiff collar with a lace insert circling her neckline and Kathryn felt she was the height of Eastern sophistication.

As this Galahad moved closer, his face broke into a grin that positively lit his chiselled features. Kathryn smiled primly back, her lashes fluttering only the merest bit. She noticed the light grey of his eyes and the dimples that bracketed his wonderful mouth.

"Beautiful!" The young man pronounced as he stood beside the carriage.

Kathryn blushed at the brashness of this stranger, although she enjoyed the flattery. "Why, thank you, sir," she replied coquettishly, the smile on her face blossoming. She was about to introduce herself when he reached out and patted the tall wheel of the phaeton.

"When I get some money scraped together, I'm getting me one of these rides." He whistled softly, and then nodded at Kathryn before going into the office. "Ma'am."

Kathryn's face flamed as realization of the true object of his admiration became obvious. "Well, of all the insolent, rude, forward..." she cursed, trying to cover her embarrassment. He must think her vain, indeed, behaving like a smitten schoolgirl. She was mortified and prayed her aunt would finish her business and they could leave before he reappeared.

The instant Aunt Belle climbed back into the wagon, Kathryn handed her the reins. "Next stop, the Carter Academy?" she inquired hastily. Any place would do as long as it was away from here. She never wanted to run into that insolent knave again.

At the mention of the Academy, Aunt Belle's face filled with sadness. "Katy, dear one, I think we should skip the school. Let's go home for a nice cup of tea."

"Nonsense. Nothing ventured, nothing gained." Kathryn reached over and gave the reins a shake of encouragement. Nellie tossed her head, still in coltish mode from their wild ride, and cantered off down the street.

THE CARTER ACADEMY WAS VERY MODERN. It was two stories and painted a dignified grey with white trim. There were tall mullioned windows, and a shiny brass bell hung in a covered alcove. On each end of the building were doors marked *Girls* and *Boys*, which seemed overly formal for this rustic town and better suited to a large city school.

Pulling the carriage to a stop, Belle jumped down and bent to inspect the horse's hoof. "I think Nellie picked up a stone. Give me a couple of minutes while I fix her up and I'll go in with you." She rummaged in the seat box for a hoof pick to remove the rock.

As Kathryn prepared herself for being turned away because she was Métis, her mixed blood started to boil. Impatience overcame prudence as she strode to the front entrance and walked in the glass doors with the gold lettering proclaiming *Carter Academy, No Peddlers*.

She marched past a polished wooden bench flanked by large aspidistra plants and headed straight for the office marked *Head Mistress*. Knocking politely, Kathryn waited to be admitted.

An austere woman opened the tall, imposing door.

"May I help you?"

Kathryn's bravado shrivelled as the woman assessed her over half-rimmed spectacles perched on a hawk-like nose.

"I would like to attend your institution and have come to enrol." Her voice sounded weak, so she straightened her spine and forced herself to meet the woman's chilly scrutiny.

Taken aback, the teacher hesitated; but, having approved Kathryn's stylish outfit and well-bred demeanour, swung the door wide. "I'm Miss Weaver, Headmistress of this institution. Come in and we can discuss this matter in a more appropriate venue."

Kathryn did her best to sound mature and ladylike during the enrolment interview, which was what she imagined a police interrogation must be like. When asked about her academic background, she held her head up a fraction higher. "My marks from Our Lady of Mercy Academy for Young Ladies in Toronto have always been exemplary and I am confident that I can pass the entrance exam for your school."

This confidence must have been interpreted as a challenge to the Headmistress, whose lips pinched tightly together – much like Sister Bernadette's when she caught you running in the hall or enjoying your dessert a little too much.

"We'll see about that." She went to an ornate oak filing cabinet and retrieved a sheaf of papers. "It so happens that I have a free period. As you feel so confident, we could get this part of the process out of the way immediately."

Kathryn had thrown down the gauntlet and was prepared to do battle. "That would be fine with me." She accepted the papers and then set to work.

It took her only twenty-five minutes to complete the questions, all of which she was sure she'd answered correctly. It had been rather elementary and she felt a wee bit superior when she returned the quiz to Miss Weaver.

Retrieving a large marking pencil, the Headmistress examined Kathryn's answers. Several times, the blood-red instrument came down and hovered like an eager axeman's blade at a beheading, then reprieve was granted and the pencil rose again.

At last, the stern examiner appeared satisfied. She tidied the pages and tapped them lightly with a bony index finger. "Adequate," she pronounced dourly. "Let me explain how the Academy works."

She then went over all the benefits of the school. The Carter Academy offered all the classes Kathryn intended to take at Our Lady of Mercy, and several more university preparatory courses she would need when she applied to the Law Society of Upper Canada.

Taking a note out of her pocket, Kathryn gave it to the teacher. "I am particularly interested in obtaining these books. Would your school library have them?" Knowing she was coming here, she'd written out a list of texts she'd need to continue her studies. Aunt Belle had been doubtful even the Carter Academy would have such specialized tomes.

The Headmistress read the list, then handed it back. "Yes, we have all those titles. This is an institution of the highest academic standards and we afford our students every opportunity to excel, which of course means providing them with all the tools they need to succeed."

Surprised, Kathryn tucked the paper back into her pocket. Perhaps the Carter Academy *could* fill the gap in her studies until she went back to Toronto. She needn't fall behind; in fact, she might even surge ahead of her spoilt-rotten, chin-wagging, gossip-mongering classmates. She began to feel excited, picturing herself going to this institution, at least for a short period.

Withdrawing a formal induction form from her drawer, Miss Weaver slid it across the desk. "You'll need to fill this out and," she squinted over the narrow spectacles, "there will be the matter of the fees."

Kathryn thought of her practically non-existent inheritance. "That won't be an issue," she assured the Headmistress, relegating this to the category of *tomorrow's headaches*.

"In that case, I'm sure you will have no problem being accepted. Your entrance exam was, to be truthful, extremely well done. You will be placed with our higher achieving students." She relaxed a fraction and Kathryn thought it a very good sign. "Since you are only fourteen, I will, of course, need your parents' consent."

At this, Kathryn remembered Aunt Belle and a flash of guilt hit her. She'd forgotten her aunt who was probably sitting on that hard wooden bench in the hallway. "Actually, my aunt is my guardian and I believe she is waiting outside."

"Wonderful. We always like to meet the family of new students." The stern instructor rose from her desk and moved toward the door. "I find you remind me of my niece. Once you're settled in, I'll make the introductions, as I think you two young ladies have a lot in common."

When Miss Weaver stepped into the hallway, she halted so abruptly that Kathryn almost ran into her.

"*This* is your aunt!" Her words were an accusation.

"Why...ah, yes. This is Miss Belle Tourond."

The Headmistress glared at Aunt Belle, with her long black braids and dark skin, then grimaced as though a large rat sat on the bench. "She's a *half breed.*" The teacher made no attempt to hide her disgust.

The insulting words were a stinging slap but Kathryn tried to keep her voice reasonable. "It is *I* that am applying to your school and you assured me there was no problem!"

The temperature in the room dropped to freezing. "Your application is rejected. We are not accepting new students at this time."

"I can get a transcript of my marks from Our Lady of Mercy and if it's about the money, I said I could pay the fees..." Kathryn hurriedly tried to cover all the objections, knowing there was nothing she could do about the obvious one.

"I said there is no room. You and *your aunt* must leave

immediately." The woman retreated to her office, slamming the door with a resounding bang.

Kathryn now understood why poisoned apples were so popular in fairy tales.

"Nellie's foot is fine and I had a nice rest waiting." Belle said quietly, and then added sympathetically, "Don't worry, Katy. I'll help with your studies at home. We'll find the books you need and maybe the Sisters at the convent school will let you write the tests and send them back in the mail."

Kathryn couldn't hide her distress. She didn't know whether to scream in outrage or weep in disappointment.

"Oh, my dear girl," Aunt Belle moved to Kathryn, giving her a comforting hug. "This is the way it is for us. Out here, we are so few, with no one to champion our cause. Life on the road allowances is not ideal, far from it, but we have to accept it and make the best life we can for our families."

Kathryn was so angry she could spit. She stared at the Headmistress's closed door and wanted to march back in and demand the bigoted woman see reason. "This is so unfair! What kind of place is this?" She fired the question at the indifferent portal rather hoping her words would be heard through the barricade, then turned to her aunt, still raging. "The law of the land is for everyone except the Métis? You have no justice or protection and no safe haven. Worse, your tarpaper existence can be burned out from under you at any time. This is *not* the Canada I was raised in. What is happening to the Ditch People is, is...nothing short of criminal!"

Her aunt, ever patient, listened to her tirade and agreed tiredly. "Yes, *ma chère*, it is unfair and yet we must survive. We who live in the road allowances discovered the hard way that raising our head for attention will only get it shot off."

"I agree, the Métis must survive," Kathryn said in as reasonable a tone as she could muster, "but at such a price? This school is the perfect example of everything that's wrong with your system. I passed that ridiculous test with flying colours and there was no question of my being accepted – no question until my race was revealed." She felt tears, hot and bitter, stinging and wanted to hit something before they spilled over and completely humiliated her. She saw the futility of it all written in the resignation on her aunt's face. Impossible!

"Come, Aunt Belle," she said stiffly. "I smell something rotten in here." And with that, Kathryn strode out of the school with her head held high and her spine poker straight.

Chapter 7

MAGIC AND MASKED MEN

After a fitful sleep, disturbed by bumps in the night, Kathryn awoke very early and decided to put the sour school experience behind her. She was now even more determined to get home to Toronto; however, after some realistic thinking and brutal calculations on not only the train fare, but necessities like clothing and tuition, Kathryn had accepted the hard fact that she would need a substantial amount of money to fund her escape. How she would come up with this money was a mystery she didn't yet know, but she would find a way.

And speaking of mysteries…Her thoughts returned once again to the Highwayman, the only truly intriguing thing about River Falls. He seemed to occupy her mind an inordinate amount of the day and sometimes the night too, when an unknown hero, tall, dark and mercilessly handsome, would come riding into her dreams.

When she became a member of the Law Society of Upper Canada, it would be her full-time job to uncover the truth. So, why not start now by uncovering who this Robin Hood of the wild west was? It would help pass the hours and develop her skills. What a coup for her to discover what no one else had been able to – the identity of the River Falls Highwayman!

Where to start? The best way to do this was to talk to her new, albeit temporary, neighbours. She would subtly question them, gleaning every bit of information she could; then, using her superior powers of deduction, put all the clues together to discover her man's identity.

Kathryn dressed quickly and tidied her small room, carefully straightening her precious books, then went to set her plan in motion. Opening the doors on the tall cupboards in the kitchen, she inspected the bottles, bags and boxes.

"What on earth are you up to, Katydid?" her aunt asked, bustling into the cabin.

Startled, Kathryn whirled around, feeling oddly off kilter. She thought she was the only one up, yet here was her aunt completely dressed, including high-laced boots wet with dew and hair neatly braided. How peculiar.

"Aunt Belle! You may as well shoot me as scare me to death!" She patted the spot over her fluttering heart for emphasis. "I thought I would get an early start on the day. I'm going to make delicious muffins for the neighbours." She turned back to the cupboard and peered at a box marked bicarbonate of soda. "As a thank you for the wonderful party we had."

Distracted, Aunt Belle moved to the peg holding her capote, a waist length coat fashioned from a Hudson's Bay blanket, grabbed it and turned for the door once more. "How thoughtful. If you wait until I get back, I can help."

It was then that Kathryn noticed she was holding a paper sack. "Get back?" The sun was barely up. "Where are you going at this hour? It can't be much past six o'clock."

"I have to take this medicine over to Mrs. Jones. I pray it will make the difference." Without waiting, Aunt Belle hurried out the door, leaving Kathryn filled with more questions than answers.

Grabbing her sweater off the back of a chair, Kathryn raced to catch up.

Aunt Belle hastily pulled a very sleepy horse out of the lean-to and, slipping her Métis sash around Nellie's neck to act as a makeshift bridle, jumped onto the horse's back, then reached down for Kathryn.

"If you're coming, then come on, girl. There's not a minute to waste."

Kathryn tentatively took the outstretched hand. She clambered awkwardly up and after much squirming and huffing, managed to seat herself behind her aunt.

"Hold on!" Belle touched her heels to the horse's sides and they were off.

At first the jostling and fast gait caused Kathryn to cling rather childishly for dear life to her aunt. Adjusting herself to a more natural position on the horse's broad back, she decided as transport, Nellie was actually rather nice, like straddling a wide carpeted log. The ride was quite comfortable, once you grew used to the movement of the strong muscles under the warm flesh.

The early morning air was crisp and clean, with an intoxicating scent of tangy pine. In fact, if it weren't for the sense of urgency, this whole excursion would have been very enjoyable. They cut across green fields and forded the river, eventually arriving at a quaint white clapboard house with a fence around the yard and sweet peas climbing a trellis over the gate.

Kathryn immediately knew this was no road allowance shanty. Sliding off Nellie, her aunt didn't wait as she rushed to the front door of the tidy house.

It was immediately opened by a young woman, worry lines aging her ashen face.

"I have medicine for Louisa," Aunt Belle stated without preamble.

The woman motioned for them to enter. "I'm so frightened, Belle. Her fever won't break and she's very weak."

The distressed mother crossed the room and knelt before a wooden cradle in which Kathryn glimpsed a tiny baby lying unnaturally still except for the jerky rise and fall of her chest as she struggled to take in a raspy breath.

"She's been sick for days. We're about out of our heads with worry."

This remark came from a rake-thin man who was dressed in a rather stuffy suit. He appeared awkward and out of place, like he was on his way to work at the bank, but had forgotten to go in. Kathryn decided he must be the baby's father and watched as he placed a shaky arm around his wife's shoulders.

Aunt Belle put the paper bag on the table and withdrew a bottle filled with white powder. "Alice, you must mix this with warm water and give it to Louisa to drink. It tastes bitter; still, we must get it into the child."

The young woman's fear etched her face. "I tried an infusion of willow bark like you said, and have been sponging her down, but nothing's working. She's going to die, isn't she, Belle, like my little Billy two years ago." She contorted in anguish as fresh tears streamed down her cheeks.

Belle put the bottle on the table and took the woman's hands in hers. "No, my dear, we must not think like that. Right now, Louisa needs us to be strong. We will give her the help she needs to get well. Together we can do this, Alice. This is a new medicine which is going to fix that baby of yours up fine. Now, get me some water and a clean cloth." Her voice was gentle, and yet there was no hint of weakness or doubt. Even Kathryn believed there was going to be a miracle.

With new vigour, Alice retrieved the necessary items as Aunt Belle picked the child up and laid her on the kitchen table. The baby didn't stir, behaving rather like a limp rag doll.

Aunt Belle took the vial of powder and mixed some into the cup of water, then dipped the cloth into the slurry and put the end into the child's mouth. Patiently, she dripped the medicine into the baby as the anxious parents hovered nearby.

When she was satisfied the infant had ingested enough of the draught, Aunt Belle wrapped baby Louisa in a blanket and returned her to the cradle. She then went to the stove and proceeded to make tea.

Kathryn was starting to think of this beverage as Métis chicken soup. All it took was the slightest problem, and out came the teapot.

They sat silently drinking the strong brew as Kathryn endlessly refilled their cups from a bottomless pot. The only noise that of the grandfather clock ticking loudly as the long minutes marched slowly by dragging the hours with them.

Without warning, the baby mewled; then Kathryn saw a pink fist thrust upward from the cradle.

The young mother rushed to her child, picking the babe up and holding her close. Then she raised her tear-stained face, wonderment replacing despair. "The fever, Belle, the fever, it's broken! She's cool to the touch and her colour is much better. God bless you!"

Belle went to examine the infant as the father stood mute witness, apparently not believing what was happening. Then everyone was laughing and hugging as the reality of the unexpected recovery became real.

Kathryn's mind swirled with questions. What was this medicine? Where had it come from?

The bottle lay forgotten on the table and Kathryn picked it up. Printed clearly on the label was one word: *Aspirin*. She'd heard about this new discovery and knew it was available only from a doctor. She also knew it was very, *very* expensive. How could Aunt Belle have come by this wonder drug?

Then she remembered the noises in her dreams, and her disturbed sleep. Had the Highwayman made a midnight delivery last night, a delivery of much needed, rare medicine? If so, this was a fairytale ending to a story that could have been heart-wrenchingly tragic. Kathryn couldn't have written a more wonderful epic: drama, fear and then, thanks to a magic elixir delivered by an unknown hero in a black mask, the baby princess saved and the kingdom rejoicing.

By the time Kathryn and Aunt Belle left, the baby had eaten, wet her diaper and was kicking and cooing like any other happy child. They bade the relieved young couple good-bye and rode back toward River Falls.

"Aunt Belle, that couple, they aren't Métis, are they?" she asked, balancing herself on Nellie's broad back. She had been trying to puzzle this out.

"No, Katydid, they aren't."

"Then why did you help them? A nice white couple like them: they could have brought the doctor out from Hopeful."

Her aunt stiffened. "I'll thank you not to talk like that,

young lady. When folks are in need, the shade of their skin is the last thing to worry about. That child was extremely ill and the old drunk they call a doctor couldn't heal anything more than a blister or a boil. Could you live with yourself if we let that baby die and kept the medicine for only our own? Katy, it doesn't matter who it is, we work together out here."

Kathryn supposed she should be quiet, but after her experience at the school, she fairly bristled. "And you can bet the doctor wouldn't make any house calls to River Falls if one of the Métis children was sick."

"And two wrongs make a right? No, *ma chère*, we must lead by example. That innocent angel didn't care what colour the person was who saved her. Maybe in the future, she will grow to an adult who will see the wisdom of being colour blind. The Métis will be here for a long time and so will the white man. We must plant the seeds and wait for the harvest."

Kathryn had nothing to say to this. Aunt Belle was right, of course. And she had been amazing during the whole ordeal, so calm and in charge, truly a pillar of strength.

In this savage land, where the rules of civilized society proved tenuous at best, it was easy to forget the ideals one had been raised to believe in. Kathryn felt ashamed of her racist remarks; she hadn't meant them.

How easy to slip into that trap.

She thought of her father. He would have been so proud of his sister; more proud of her than of his daughter.

There was still one mystery. "Aunt Belle, where did you get the Aspirin? I read about it back east, but as far as I know, it's a special thing indeed."

Casually swatting at a horsefly, her aunt dismissed the question. "Where it came from is not important, Katydid, what matters is that we had it in time. Sometimes Providence steps in and delivers what we need."

Providence, or a masked stranger who procured it gratis from a hospital somewhere, Kathryn thought as they rode on in the warm noonday sun.

Chapter 8

A LORD, A LADY AND ALADDIN'S LAMP

Once they arrived back at the cabin, Aunt Belle busied herself as though nothing unusual had happened.

"What kind are you going to make?" she asked, slipping her apron on, then pulling bags marked *flour* and *sugar* from the tall cupboard and placing them on the table.

"Kind?" Kathryn needed a second to catch up.

"Yes, kind of muffins."

Kathryn noted the growing pile of what she guessed would be needed ingredients, none of which she had the faintest idea how to use. She didn't want her aunt to know she'd used up all her culinary talents when she'd made tea and re-heated the bannock. "Ah, I'm not sure. What would you suggest?"

Her aunt thought for a moment. "Hmm, as far as ingredients go, muffins take a lot, and you won't end up with a large number to share. How about thimble cookies instead? The same amount of basics will go a lot further and I have several jars of raspberry jam you can use."

"That sounds perfect." Kathryn hadn't a clue what came next.

"What would you like me to do?" Her aunt indicated the stove. "I could fire up the oven."

"Good thinking. We certainly will need a fiery oven." Kathryn removed her sweater, hanging it on a peg next to Aunt Belle's shawl and tried to imagine how one made a thimble cookie. "And I guess we'll need a, a..."

Aunt Belle waited expectantly.

"A...a thimble!" Kathryn blurted triumphantly.

Her aunt gave her a knowing smile. "You haven't any idea how to make cookies, do you?"

"Actually, cookie cooking has a pretty low rung on my academic ladder. I don't plan on being a pastry chef." Kathryn didn't want to say what she truly dreamed of being, as it invariably brought snickers. Her classmates equated aspiring to become a barrister with wanting to be Queen of the British Empire or Czarina of all the Russias.

"You do know how to do the basics like bake bread?" Aunt Belle asked cautiously.

Kathryn shook her head.

"How about cook a moose pot roast and make gravy?"

Again, Kathryn demurred.

"Mon Dieu! Can you poach an egg, child?"

This was like speaking a foreign language to Kathryn. "Eat, yes; cook no."

Aunt Belle then did a remarkable thing. She hugged

her niece warmly. "When I was a girl, I had a lot of trouble with cooking too. My mother had serious doubts I would survive without her. If you like, I could teach you?"

"Me? Cook?" Kathryn had never thought about this. She supposed it would be a worthwhile talent to have; after all, even lady lawyers had to eat. "That would be much appreciated."

For the next hour, Kathryn was instructed on how to measure and sift the flour, whisk the eggs, chop nuts and make the deep dimple that would hold the jam in the cookies.

By the time they finished the lesson, Kathryn had a whole new respect for anything baked, toasted, chopped, fried, boiled or blanched. Never before had she considered how the meals she ate were prepared. She assumed there was a process with pots and ovens, measuring and peeling, but at her elite school, young ladies were not allowed into the scullery and the food had simply come out of the kitchens and appeared in front of her.

Kathryn placed the last batch of cookies on the table, and then wiped her forehead. "Impossible!"

Aunt Belle's approval was obvious as she inspected the dozens of golden brown jewels spread out across the table. "To celebrate your first cooking class, I'll clean up while you deliver these to our neighbours."

"I can't turn down an offer like that!" Kathryn agreed as she surveyed the mess the kitchen was in. She was also

eager to move on to the second step of her cunning plan –
gathering information and pertinent clues. After the
Aspirin episode, in which Aunt Belle had been so stingy
with her information, Kathryn's curiosity had taken
control. She needed answers, which meant asking the right
questions.

After carefully wrapping the cookies in waxed paper,
Kathryn set out to distribute her goodies and in the process,
discover as much as possible about the Highwayman.

Although the people were extremely surprised and
grateful at her offering, the first four households Kathryn
visited did nothing to help solve the mystery. Each time,
she drank cups and cups of tea as she listened to the many
stories about this wonderful phantom. With each telling,
he grew larger; still, no one knew who he was. It was not
until she got to Madame Garnier's cobbled cottage that
things started improving.

"*Le Bandit de Grand Chemin! Un homme mystérieux,
oui?* He comes and goes; no one knows where he lives.
Sometimes, he disappears for weeks at a time, then *voila!*
Like magic, he appears when he is needed most," Madame
Garnier offered enthusiastically. "He is the sword of justice,
sent by God, I am sure."

Kathryn filed this information away. The Highwayman would disappear for weeks at a time and reappear
without warning and no one knew where he lived.

Her next stop yielded no new information and she was

fast running out of cookies. With only two batches left, Kathryn hoped she would come up with something special to help track down this legend known as the Highwayman. She turned into the lane that led to Madame Thibault's. As she walked up to the ramshackle house, she couldn't believe what she saw. Two very young boys – for they could be no more than five and seven – were throwing knives into the dirt at each other's feet, which were perilously close to the blades.

"You there, you boys! What on earth do you think you're doing? Stop that, this instant." Kathryn stamped her own foot for emphasis. She wondered where the boys' mother was and why she didn't make these naughty children cease this insanity before one of them lost a toe.

The youngest was speechless, and his elder brother gave her a foul glare. "Why should we stop? We're not doing anything wrong," he protested.

"I hardly think flinging knives at each other is sanctioned by your parents," Kathryn used her most mature voice, sure the boys heard the authority in it.

"Papa lets us play *la petite patou*." His head went up proudly and with more than a little defiance. "He says every Métis should know how to throw a knife and this game is a fun way to learn."

The boy crossed his arms in what Kathryn could only call righteous indignation. She didn't know what to say. Some of the customs she'd discovered in River Falls were completely bizarre, but if they were to grow up hunters, she supposed being familiar with a deadly blade made sense. After all, she was a stranger and could make an honest mistake through simple ignorance. Perhaps she had been the tiniest bit hasty.

Kathryn sniffed. "Oh well, if your parents know, carry on."

Feeling rather foolish, she whisked by them and went to the door of the house, which stood open.

"Hello?" Kathryn knocked tentatively. "It's me, Kathryn Tourond; I met you at Madame Ducharme's."

The lady of the house waved her in. "Of course, come in, my dear."

Kathryn stepped into a world of carved wooden toys, piles of folded laundry and general mayhem as two small boys raced past her waving sticks.

"Please, have a seat." Madame Thibault motioned toward the kitchen table as she wiped her hands on her smeared apron. "I have only this minute poured the water for tea. I like a strong cup so we'll wait for it to steep."

Before Kathryn could protest that she'd already had more than enough of the black brew for today, the cups were set out and her fate sealed.

The harried mother shooed the boisterous boys outside. "Go and play swords with your brothers. There are dangerous dragons outside and I'm sure they need slaying."

Kathryn sat, resigned to another cup of tea, and explained why she had come. "I wanted to say thank you for the wonderful welcoming party and thought a sweet treat filled the bill. Unfortunately, my baking skills are not what they should be." She thought 'humble,' (however undeserved as each cookie had been inspected and found perfect), would make her seem more approachable. Smiling sweetly, she took a dozen of the morsels out of her basket and placed them on an empty plate.

Madame Thibault laughed. "Oh, my dear child, you are most welcome. I have yet to meet a Métis who doesn't love to listen to the fiddle and your arrival supplied an excuse to get together and rosin up the bow. It is we who should be thanking you and as for the cookies, my herd of boys wouldn't care if they were cinders, they would still gobble them down and look for more."

As she sipped her tea and discussed the weather, her life in Toronto, and other safe topics, Kathryn eased back to the subject she was dying to find out more about. "While I was chatting with two lovely gentlemen, I heard tell of a man who does daring exploits on behalf of the folks at River Falls – robbing from the rich and giving to the poor; righting wrongs, that sort of thing. He sounded very interesting and I wonder if you knew anything about him."

"The Highwayman, oh yes, he is a genuine hero. I shudder to think where we would be without that angel. Sadly, I don't know anything more to tell you."

This was not what Kathryn wanted to hear. She had given out a lot of cookies without discovering many clues.

Plus, she had imbibed an ocean of tea which had led to her visiting more outhouses than she cared to count!

After her goodbyes, Kathryn was leaving when she spied another of the Thibault clan dangling from a nearby poplar. Even upside down, he was familiar and as she got closer, she realized she'd seen this particular jester before. It was the lad with the scarlet chapeau, her Prairie Puss in Boots.

The memory of how she'd rebuffed him at the dance made her cringe. She hadn't meant to be so rude, and to add to that insult, she couldn't seem to dredge up his name. She tried to recall it and remembered it was something odd, like numbers or...

"JP!" She blurted rather loudly as it came back to her in the nick of time. It was an odd way of referring to him and she wondered what the initials stood for.

He immediately swung up to a sitting position on the branch he'd been hanging from. "Aye, I am that Lord of Renown, Kate, and verily, I am glad to see you again, fair damsel."

His manner was so friendly; she decided he wasn't the type to hold a grudge. She would play along with his courtly mannerisms. "Thou art truly a kind liege, sire. And the name is Kathryn, as in 'Kathryn' the Great."

An old expression used by one of the Sisters at the convent school came into her head. *Little pitchers have big ears*, meaning children often overhear from grown-ups things that they shouldn't. She doubted this strange boy would have a problem with misappropriating the occasional kernel of information, whatever the source. "Your Majesty, I was having tea with your royal mother, and we were speaking of a fellow called the Highwayman. I don't suppose you know anything about this auspicious knight?"

He reacted as though that was the dumbest thing he'd ever heard. "Of course. I know all the details about every one of my loyal subjects and everything that happens in my kingdom."

Kathryn sized up the wiry lad, recognising the intelligence in his lively face. "Yes, I bet you do. Pray tell me about this Highwayman."

"What's it worth to you?" All business now, he folded his arms across his chest as he sat perched high above.

Kathryn was taken aback. She supposed after the way she'd refused him at the dance, she had this one coming. "What about a feast fit for a palace banquet?"

"Depends." There was a mischievous light in his brown eyes. "What do you offer, comely peasant girl?"

Kathryn held up the basket. "My liege, I offer a prize worth more than all the jewels in your kingdom. I bring golden delicacies, prepared with the finest ingredients in the royal kitchens and they would be entirely for you, since none of your loyal subjects are around to demand their share of the loot."

Grabbing his feathered hat which had been propped on the branch next to him, JP jumped from the tree.

Plunking himself down on a stump, he carefully placed the hat on his head at a rakish angle then beckoned her forward. "You may approach the throne and present your offerings."

She moved closer, curtsied gracefully and opened the basket, revealing the fragrant contents.

He sniffed appreciatively and Kathryn knew she had him. You could always count on a boy's stomach to win in a fight. Reaching out a less than clean hand, JP made to filch one of the cookies.

She snatched the basket back. "Not so fast, sire. Preceding your enjoying this bountiful harvest, I need to know what information you have."

He winked at her and she quirked a brow at him.

"The noble knight we speak of fights for my serfs in my stead. As sovereign of this land, I am not allowed to put my life in jeopardy."

"That makes perfect sense, your majesty." Kathryn was enjoying the pantomime.

"He is summoned when needed and defends the down trotten."

"Trodden," Kathryn corrected, allowing him to retrieve one morsel from the basket.

"Forsooth, that's what I said," He stood, brandishing the cookie like a miniscule shield. "And astride his midnight steed, our ebony-haired knight vanquishes his foe with his ivory hilted dagger."

Kathryn narrowed her eyes, this was interesting. "Ivory...his knife has an ivory handle!"

"Aye; and, wrong-handed he saves the day every night." With this the shield disappeared into JP's mouth.

Kathryn tried to unravel what he meant. *"Saves the day every night?"*

He bristled at her constant correcting before continuing in his best *ye olde English*. "Verily, the Highwayman performs these jousts under cover of darkness, so he shan't be nabbed by Constable Dung."

"By this, you mean Constable Blake?" She was catching on.

"He has been known in the realm by that name, but I like mine better."

"And what do you mean by *wrong handed*, sire?"

"He uses the *wrong* hand when he throws his knife," JP patiently explained as though she were slow witted. "He's a lefty."

Kathryn mulled this over. She now knew the Highwayman was not always around, and when he showed up, he rode a dark horse, carried a knife with an ivory hilt, was left-handed and had black hair.

"You are wise and knowledgeable." She regarded him knowingly. "And methinks thou readest books..." She had his undivided attention now. "And those books have dragons and knights, wizards and witches.... Treasures beyond imagining."

He leaned toward her and when she saw the eagerness in his brown eyes; the sparks swirling within showed her that he coveted books as much as she. Kathryn had not expected someone from these dispossessed people to have such a strong love of reading. "I have *treasures* stashed at my aunt's house. As a reward for imparting your information to me, I would share those treasures as I know you would value them more than gold, as do I."

He reacted like a child on Christmas morning. "Really! Truly? You mean it, Kate?"

He jumped up from his throne so quickly, that Kathryn laughed. He was practically dancing now.

"Under two conditions..." She hesitated, waiting to see if he would accept her offer.

"Yes, sure, name your price."

"That you call me Kathryn and..." She paused, drawing out the suspense. "I don't think you were christened JP. I would like to know your real name."

This made him stop. "*JP* is what I am known by and *JP* is what I answer to."

She thought about it, and then decided giving in was a way of making up for the slight at the dance. "Then JP is what I'll call you."

"Personally, I can't stand my name and it's one piece of information I never share."

She bobbed her head. "I can respect that and the offer of the books stands, JP."

"You have no idea what this means to me. Thank you, Kathryn. I've been reading the same two books for years now as my papa said there was no money for frivolities and to him, books are frivolities. You've saved me!"

Kathryn dipped into her deepest curtsey. "For my King of the Scarlet Chapeau, only the best will do."

"I shall make the pilgrimage and promise thy wondrous book shall be guarded by all the knights in my kingdom. Adieu, fair lady." With a flourish, he swept his colourful hat from his head and bowed, then took his leave.

Kathryn waved goodbye. Thanks to JP, she could begin her search.

IT WAS THE MIDDLE OF THE NIGHT and aggravatingly, Kathryn still tossed and turned, sleep evading her. She fluffed her blonde hair across the pillow, arranging it artfully, then lay back and crossed her arms over her chest, like a beautiful, pale corpse. If she died tonight, they would find her still body, as perfect as Sleeping Beauty waiting for her prince, serene in death as she never was while alive on this cursed night. After a while she gave up on the cadaver pose, punched her pillow into submission and flopped back down. The mystery of who the masked hero might be ran through her head, vexing her with the tantalizing clues she'd been given by the boy, JP. In truth, he was not such a boy, but near her own age; still, it was hard to think of her prairie puss as a young man.

She'd been comparing all the neighbours she'd met with the list of things she now knew about the Highwayman. She wished she'd paid more attention when she'd been introduced to the citizens of River Falls so she could start matching clues to suspects. In her defence, who noticed details like ivory handled knives? She was sure that the Highwayman must be a Métis, as who else would so staunchly defend the Ditch People? So who were the candidates? Her mind flew back to her early days at River Falls as she reviewed the possible perpetrators.

The first deed done by the Highwayman was when Pierre had his painting problem with Mr. Campbell. He had a great motive for revenge after the hardware merchant refused to pay, but then he'd been compensated with the stolen paint and oats delivered under cover of darkness by the mysterious Highwayman.

What if Pierre broke into the hardware store and stole the goods then in order to throw suspicion in a different direction, he'd created the ruse of the Highwayman to cover his tracks? He could continue righting wrongs and no one would suspect him since he was already a recipient of the masked benefactor's justice.

That was so clever and devious it was something Kathryn could have come up with herself.

And what of Joseph? He'd said he was always tearing around the countryside in search of ingredients for his wife's bakery. That would allow him to gather information and be in different locations to perform his Robin Hood-ish deeds with no one the wiser.

She wasn't going to exclude Francis either. True, with his ruined right hand, he was not the obvious choice for the Bandit de Grand Chemin except Kathryn had seen how well he functioned when he hung her door. He could easily be her *wrong handed bandit*.

In addition, there were those Métis who didn't live in River Falls, like Henri Beauchamp who was saved from eating gophers by this phantom hero. No one would know what Henri was up to since he wasn't part of the community and when he needed to steal food, what better subterfuge than to blame it on his own creation, the Highwayman. Sure, he'd passed along some of the goods, but it was a small price to ensure his family wasn't dining on vermin.

Solving this puzzle would require someone with the skills of that popular detective Sherlock Holmes to deduce who was their culprit.

The whole thing had given her a terrible throbbing headache and exhausted Kathryn drifted into an uneasy sleep. Her dreamscape swirled with gauzy mist. Ahead, through the vapour, she saw her parents watching her. She ran to catch up, never coming close enough to touch them. Why didn't they stay? The more she chased them, the angrier she became.

And then her dream world spun her into her lumpy

old bed in the dormitory at the convent school. She had a crucial mathematics exam to study for, but an annoying pounding sound, like distant hoof beats, distracted her from memorizing the nine times table.

A noise roused her and Kathryn rolled over, her groggy mind trying to determine if the sound originated in her dream world or the real one. She dismissed it and was about to try to recapture sleep when she was startled by a strange illumination flooding the narrow crack beneath her bedroom door. She tried to make sense of what she was seeing. A lantern was yellow, but this light was crimson. How strange! Kathryn wondered what was going on.

Dragging herself out of her soft bed, she stumbled half asleep to her bedroom door in time to see her aunt silently leaving. It was only a glimpse as the cabin door closed, but it seemed the lantern she held did glow an unearthly red colour. Kathryn immediately thought of Aladdin and his wondrous Lamp which held a magic genie within.

Her aunt had mentioned there'd been a bear around. Perhaps the strange red light didn't attract the animal or better still, scared it away. Kathryn massaged her still-throbbing temples. "Well, if we have to use that accursed latrine for night visits, Aunt Belle could have warned me to use the special lamp." Yawning, she vowed not to make any more midnight trips before speaking to her aunt about tonight's discovery and gratefully, she returned to her warm bed.

Chapter 9

RED RIDING HOOD
FINDS THE HOLY GRAIL

When Aunt Belle asked her to pick raspberries the next morning, Kathryn hesitated. This would be another new experience which, she'd discovered with the mud and straw lesson, could be nasty indeed.

The problem with refusing was that her aunt may come up with some other odious chore, like scrubbing the floors or dusting for spider webs. Berry picking may be the least of today's evils.

"Thanks for doing this, Katy. I have to finish an important sewing project or I'd go with you. One question: are you sure you're up to it?" Her aunt handed her an empty bucket.

Kathryn snorted derisively. "Please, Aunt Belle. It's only picking berries! How hard could it be?" And with that, she waltzed out of the cabin, swinging the pail and feeling like Little Red Riding Hood on her way to grandma's house.

The berry patch her aunt sent her to turned out to be as impenetrable as any castle guarded by fire-belching dragons.

Cursing, Kathryn pushed her way through the thorny brambles, batting at the prickly branches. There weren't many berries to be had, still she persisted and managed to pluck the occasional dark red prize. The price was steep. He arms were scratched and sweat ran down her back as she thrust at a particularly nasty bush. The apron she'd slid over her dress was torn in several places and she doubted her shoes would ever be the same.

"O-o-o-w-w-w!" Shrieking, Kathryn snatched at her hair which had become entangled with a twig and was being viciously yanked from her scalp. She fought to free herself, but the harder she pulled, the tighter the tenacious branch bound her.

She was truly caught, snared, doomed. They would find her bleached bones, hanging from the bramble's deadly thorns. This would never have happened if she were back in Toronto. She could send the maid or the kitchen staff to fetch a berry if she really needed one.

Frantically, Kathryn jiggled the barbed bush, to no avail. She twisted her neck to see if she could untie the knotted hair, but it only wound her closer.

She needed Sir Giles to ride in and chop the vines away, freeing her from this peril. It struck her that perhaps there was someone else picking berries on the other side of this horrid patch. They could save her. "Hello, anyone out there?"

Silence. The only sound was that of the warm breeze, laughing softly at her as it rippled through the tall prairie grass.

Kathryn remembered the bear lurking about. And what did bears eat? Why, juicy red raspberries, of course. And would Mr. Bear be angry at her for invading his lunch box? Why, yes he would!

She could be in serious danger.

"Help!" She screamed this time. "I need help!"

"You've really got yourself in a peck of trouble."

Startled, Kathryn twisted trying to see who'd spoken, allowing the thorn she'd been avoiding to bite into her cheek and she winced. She remembered feeling like Little Red Riding Hood when she'd left this morning and hoped this wasn't the Big Bad Wolf.

There was the sound of bushes being cut and branches snapping; then the gleam of a knife blade flashed, slicing down close to her head!

She almost fainted, sure that the end had come at last.

And then the branch that had captured her fell away and she was free. She backed out of the berry patch, the twig still dangling from her bedraggled hair. Her face was bleeding, the apron torn and sweat ran down her face. Once away from the savage bushes, she gratefully turned to meet her Sir Galahad.

Gratitude became mortification as Kathryn stared into the grey eyes of the young man she'd seen while in the Phaeton. It all came back to her in excruciating detail – her coquettish simpering, his interest in a vehicle over her. Her life was a series of disasters since coming to this Godforsaken prairie. Frustrated, she smacked at the branch, still hanging limply from its hair noose.

Her rescuer moved a little closer. "Here, let me help you."

Awkwardly, he worked her hair free. It took several minutes and a lot of teeth gritting on both their parts. Finally, the offending shrubbery was disentangled.

"There you go, Miss. You might think about wearing a big ol' hat next time." He presented her with the branch, then started to walk away.

A hat! What an impertinent thing to say! She snapped the offensive stick in two and flung it into the berry patch. "Stupid, stupid, *stupid!*" she cursed.

He stopped, turning back to her. "You talking to me?"

"No, no, not you. Please wait." Kathryn hurried over to him. "I'm sorry. We keep meeting in, well, peculiar circumstances." She held out her hand. "I'm Kathryn, not Katy, Katydid or Kate, just plain Kathryn."

"From what I see, there's nothing plain about you." He smiled and instantly, her heart melted like a crystal snowflake in the sun. "My name's Mark."

Touching the side of her head, Kathryn casually felt for a bald spot, praying it wasn't as bad as she thought. "I had no idea I'd have so much trouble with one little berry picking excursion." She showed him her mostly empty pail and sighed loudly. "I guess my raspberry pie baking will have to wait."

"It's a might early for berries." Mark held up a tin box.

"I was going to have lunch down by the river. Would you like to share mine?"

"Your lunch?"

"My pie. It's apple and my ma makes the best in the world."

How could she refuse this Lancelot anything?

Kathryn had never spent such a pleasant afternoon. They sat on the riverbank under the shade of a spreading poplar and ate Mark's sizable lunch, including a huge wedge of pie, which lived up to its billing. It was delicious.

Although he was several years older, they still found all manner of things to talk about. Everything Mark said totally fascinated Kathryn and she listened mesmerized. He liked pigs and planned on having the biggest hog operation this side of Winnipeg. He'd already won several ribbons at the county fair with his prize sow.

"How interesting!" Kathryn giggled. She hoped she sounded charming. "And what's this prize piggy's name, or do you give pigs names?"

"Oh, yeah, I name all my meals," Mark guffawed.

They were stretched out on their stomachs, watching the languid green water drift past. He leaned in toward her, bringing with him his strong, male scent. "Actually, I did name one. I call her Fatsow. Get it, Fatsow, like Fatso on account of she's such a big porker."

Kathryn burst out laughing, snorting in a very unlady-like manner, which made Mark laugh too.

"You know, that's exactly what Fatsow sounds like when it's feed time at the trough."

Kathryn tried to stifle the porcine noise by covering her mouth. She had to get control before he thought her a complete buffoon, but as she wiped the drool from her chin, she wondered if that ship had sailed.

Instead of shying away, Mark reached out and pushed a lock of her snarled hair behind her ear. "I like you, Just Plain Kathryn. You're funny."

At that moment, movement downstream caught Kathryn's eye. A horse and rider were flying along the old trail that led into the woods. Kathryn immediately recognised the cream-coloured *capote*, with its vibrant red, yellow, green and indigo stripes at the bottom. It was Aunt Belle galloping at breakneck speed on old Nellie. The startling thing was the rest of her aunt's apparel. Under the open coat which flapped in the wind, Kathryn saw she had on a chambray shirt and denim dungarees. This, along with the shortened capote made her appear quite manly. Why would she need such insane haste simply to deliver the sewing she'd been working on?

"Someone's hell-bent for leather." Mark watched for a moment; then amazement filled his face. "Why, lookie there. It's a gal and she can really ride. Who'd have thought a female could manage a horse like that."

The last comment irked Kathryn. Were women somehow incapable of riding proficiently? Maybe Mark simply didn't understand that women, given the chance and the training, could do anything and do it well.

Once they knew each other a little better, she'd have to enlighten him – substantially, but for now, she'd be as sweet and ladylike as possible. "My, that is entirely too hard for me," she said demurely. "I'd rather use a buggy, so my skirts don't get all horsey smelling." She thought that sounded sufficiently feminine.

"You're right, little lady. I think women should stay focussed on something more suitable, something they can handle, like cooking and raising children."

Kathryn tried biting her tongue to keep quiet, and then worried she'd have to clamp down so hard she'd take the end off. "Oh, I think women can *handle* a little more than baking pies and washing diapers. In fact, I think women are the equal of men and perhaps, if men weren't so afraid of how capable women are, they'd let them into professions where they aren't welcomed now!" She crossed her arms and watched Aunt Belle disappear into the woods. "And yes, that woman can ride *as well as any man*."

Mark didn't seem to get her point, patting her arm as though she were feeble-brained to have wild thoughts like those.

"Must be one of those road allowance half-breeds from down by the river. They been busy clearing all that land and planting crops. I figure that quarter section would make one swell place for my hog operation." He sucked air in through his teeth. "Yes siree, mighty fine and the price is right."

Kathryn wasn't sure what he meant. Aunt Belle had told her the Métis didn't own their land, so who was selling? There were dozens of families living in River Falls and she was pretty sure none of them would be willing to move to make room for a pig farm.

He stood and then, grabbing her hand, yanked her up in a less than gentlemanly fashion. She forgave him. Proper etiquette was something else she'd educate him on once they were, dare she say it, betrothed.

"I'd like to stay, problem is, I got chores I left undone. I'd best get to 'em."

Kathryn saw from the angle of the sun that it was indeed late. Where had the time gone?

He continued to hold her hand. "It's been...right nice."

She couldn't agree more, although she didn't know exactly how to say this and still retain her ladylike demureness, or what was left of it. Instead, she bobbled her head up and down like some demented cuckoo clock. "Nice," she echoed in agreement.

Walking home alone along the dusty road, Kathryn thought of her time with Mark. True, he had a few rough edges. That remark about woman being good only for cooking and raising children still steamed her, and some of his other comments were certainly disturbing, but he simply needed polishing and perhaps a good dose of educating. She'd help him see where he'd been wrong.

She was sure he liked her. He'd said so, hadn't he? And yes, when she was a member of the Law Society, it would be a little unusual to introduce her husband, 'the pig farmer,' but what did it matter, *a rose by any other name...*

Her hand still tingled where he'd touched her, but it was more than that. He had made her feel so, so....womanly. And he was gorgeous. In fact, he was fairytale handsome. Kathryn held her bucket out in front of her, imagining she was at the ball, waltzing with her Prince Charming while all those ugly stepsisters looked on enviously.

She now understood the Knights of the Round Table and their passion to find the Holy Grail. She'd found her grail. It walked and talked, came with brown hair and grey eyes and was called Mark!

Chapter 10

CLUES ANSWERED
AND QUESTIONS ASKED

When Kathryn arrived back at the cabin, she was surprised to see Claude Remy waiting. "Aunt Belle isn't home," she called as she walked up the path.

The afternoon sun shining on the big man's hair made it gleam blue-black.

Unbidden, the clues JP had told her about the Highwayman sprang into her head. *"And astride his midnight steed, our ebony knight vanquishes his foe wrong-handed with his ivory hilted dagger."*

Since Claude Remy was away trapping much of the time, she'd never considered him as a candidate to be the famous Highwayman. Thinking about it now...didn't that make him even more eligible? Madame Garnier had said, *"The Bandit de Grand Chemin.... He comes and goes; no one knows where he lives. Sometimes, he disappears for weeks at a time, then voila! Like magic, appears when he is needed most."* Claude came and went at odd times as he had to check his trap lines. This gave him much more opportunity than some of her other suspects. For fun, she thought she would see how many of JP's criteria old Claude chalked up.

With his long black hair and bushy beard, he certainly had the right coloration. In fact, even his dark skin could be considered as adding to the picture.

Clue number one: *ebony knight*. Check!

"Would you like a cup of tea?" she offered sweetly, trying to think of how to discover if he matched the rest of the list.

"Non." Claude's gravelly voice was gruff and he was back in full trapper style with worn trousers, a much-patched cotton shirt with a felted wool vest on top and knee-high moccasins that laced up the front. The beautifully beaded coat was nowhere to be seen or, thankfully, smelled.

Kathryn peered about. "Did you walk here, Mr. Remy?"

His reaction told her he thought she'd lost her mind. "Fool, of course not. My horse, she is tied up."

He tipped his chin in the direction of the trees where Kathryn saw a dark bay mare. The horse's coat was a rich, deep brown, very, *very* deep brown indeed, which at night could appear black.

Clue number two: *midnight steed*. Check, again!

Next was how to discover if he was left-handed? As casually as possible, Kathryn stooped to pick up a rock and then moved closer to her suspect. With a quick flip of her wrist, she tossed the stone toward the unsuspecting woodsman. "Think fast!"

He caught it with neither his right nor his left hand. The rock simply bounced off his broad chest and fell to the dirt.

"*Sacrebleu!*" he roared. "You idiot!"

"Oh, I'm so sorry. It slipped." Kathryn tried to appear contrite.

He continued cursing, switching between English, French, Cree and Michif as he strode past her and up the veranda steps to the cabin door.

"Wait! You can't go in there. I said my aunt was not at home." Kathryn ran to catch up as Claude charged on oblivious to her shouts. Acting as though he owned the place, he barged right in and deposited himself rather unceremoniously in a chair at the kitchen table.

Kathryn scurried after him. So much for finding out if he was *wrong-handed*. If she was clever, she could still discover if he owned that special knife. She'd noticed as he bulled by her that he had a scabbard hanging from his belt. Unfortunately, the knife hilt was hidden under his vest. All she needed was a peek.

Having eaten the few berries she'd picked, she deposited her empty bucket in the dry sink, then went to the potato bin, pulled several out and set them onto the table next to where the trapper sat. "Aunt Belle should be home soon. Right now, I have to get these peeled for supper." She pretended to search for something to peel with. "Oh, dear! I can't seem to find my knife. Maybe I could borrow yours!"

And with that, she lunged forward and yanked Claude's vest up, exposing the knife protruding from the sheath.

It wasn't ivory. The haft was made out of deer antler with an intricate design etched into it. The image was disturbing, a wolf's head with demonic eyes that pierced straight through you. Kathryn flinched. Would antler be considered ivory to those trying to romanticize their hero?

"You are mad, girl!" Claude shrieked in what she thought was a rather high voice for such a big man. Jumping to his feet, he knocked over the chair. "Tell Belle I have da goods." And with that, he fled the cabin.

The blade had been on his right side. Did that mean he was right-handed or left? Not having a lot of experience with trappers, let alone eight-inch hunting knives, she wasn't sure. In all her books with knights carrying swords, they carried their blade on the opposite side so they could draw it and slash the pesky varlets a good one. If knives were the same, that did indeed mean Claude was left, or wrong, handed. Check!

At the beginning of today's *Fishing-for-a-Highwayman*, Claude Remy hadn't even been in the running for the Bandit du Grand Chemin. Now, she saw how that had been short-sighted on her part.

Her mind continued to tally the clues. There was one more she had not taken into account. Aunt Belle herself had supplied this piece of the puzzle when Claude had shown up with the dead deer. *"Wherever that hidden camp of yours is, you should think about finding the nearest barber before coming back to civilization.*"

A hidden camp! Every hero needed a sanctuary. Didn't Robin Hood and his band of Merry Men have a secret hideout in Sherwood Forest?

As Kathryn watched the angry hunter ride away, she decided today had been a very interesting one indeed.

WHEN AUNT BELLE CAME HOME, Kathryn was sitting at the kitchen table reading, the potatoes in a pot on the stove. She'd prepared a large number of the vegetables as the silly things shrank at an astounding rate while she'd hacked away in her attempt to peel them.

"Mr. Remy dropped by earlier." She'd go into detail if asked, but would rather avoid explaining the testing session. "He said to tell you he *had the goods.*" It was then that she wondered what goods could her aunt have ordered from the unmannered man. She was still appalled at how he'd marched right into the cabin without knocking, as though he did it every day.

"Don't worry about Claude. He'll be back." Her aunt placed a pie on the table, then went to the cupboard and retrieved an apron. "Did you have any luck with your berry picking?"

Kathryn thought of the disastrous foray and the attack of the dragon talon bushes. "Not much." Then she remembered her time with Mark. "It was a lovely day anyway."

"Yes, I thought it might be a little early in the season. I've been craving fresh raspberries and was hoping there'd be enough for a couple of tarts. Fortunately, we can save our disappointment for another day. Madame Rousseau paid for my services with this delicious rhubarb pie. A very good deal, *n'est-ce pas?*" She arched a brow. "In fact, what do you say to a cup of tea and a big piece right now, Katydid? Who says we have to wait until after supper for dessert!"

Kathryn laughed. "You'll get no argument from me, Madame!"

As she watched her aunt preparing the tea, her thoughts drifted back to the afternoon's encounter with her Sir Galahad, Mark. She still planned on returning to Toronto as soon as possible, but he was so wonderful and for the time she had left here, she wouldn't mind a little wonderful.

Fetching plates from the china cabinet, Kathryn sliced two large pieces of the pie while her aunt poured.

As they ate the unexpected treat, Kathryn felt the long day's activities catching up with her and she yawned. "An interrupted sleep always leaves me exhausted the next day. I never feel rested. Do you find that same problem?"

Her aunt watched the tea leaves swirling in the bottom of her cup.

"And that trick you used with the lantern so the bear wouldn't find you was clever. You should have told me about it too. I sometimes have to make a midnight dash and it would have been good to know."

Her aunt meticulously forked up the last crumbs of her pie.

Kathryn continued. "Last night.... You went to the outhouse using that strange red lantern..."

"Hmm. A red lantern would be strange indeed." Aunt Belle dismissed it with a light laugh. "Maybe you were dreaming, Katydid."

Kathryn paused. Dreaming? *Dreaming!* Had she been dreaming when she'd glimpsed the lantern's light? That was all it had been, a glimpse. She had been half asleep and she did have an extraordinary headache when she'd retired. It could have triggered the red dream. "Well, it seemed very real to me..."

"Dreams can be that way, dear."

Then, without another word, Aunt Belle stood, gathered their dishes and went to the sink, leaving Kathryn in some doubt as to what she had seen. There *had* been times when her imagination had...well, caused her to leap to unfortunate conclusions. Once, she had accused a student of sneaking out to meet a boy, sure that they were planning to elope to Budapest because the girl was in a family way. The young lady in question had merely been cadging an illicit cigarette. Kathryn had ended up in Mother Superior's office, and no one had sat with her at meals for a month.

Chapter 11

PIRATE TREASURE
FROM A BANDIT

All through the next day, Kathryn's mind circulated among three thoughts: her encounter with Mark, the possibility of Claude Remy being the Highwayman, and the mystery of the red lantern.

"Katy, would you be a dear and take these to Kokum's with my compliments?"

Kathryn had been busily washing dishes, but turned at the sound of her aunt's voice and recoiled. Her aunt held out two dead fish, their glassy eyes staring balefully at the afterworld.

She shuddered. "You want me to take those all the way to Madam Ducharme's? How am I to do that?" The idea of touching the fish was positively repulsive.

Her aunt shook the fish, causing the light to bounce off their iridescent scales. "These two are past biting and in this heat, the sooner they're delivered the better."

Kathryn frantically cast about, then spied her salvation.

Grabbing the wash basin, she ran to the door and flung the soapy water into the bushes. Returning, she held out the empty dish.

Her aunt placed the fish in the large bowl, then went to a bucket and ladled cold water over them. "That should help keep the little fellows fresh. Now go, and don't forget to bring the basin back, you silly girl."

Kathryn started on the long trip to deliver her cargo. As she carefully made her way down the rough road, the afternoon sun gilded the dust motes swirling in the languid heat. It was a long walk to Madame Ducharme's shanty and the stones poked at her tender feet through the thin soles of her shoes. She would have to find something more serviceable if she was condemned to stay here much longer. She must be something to behold, the dishpan thrust out in front of her as though it held a royal feast and not two smelly dead things.

Kathryn mulled over the mystery of the red light as she walked. Assuming it was real, she would have to dismiss the idea of it being a bruin warning – Aunt Belle would have informed her if it were a safety lamp. So why deny it? What was the big secret? Why did people usually use lanterns? For light, of course; and maybe for heat and to signal messages.

She stumbled in the middle of the road, nearly dropping the fish. What if the red lantern was real, and it and the Highwayman were somehow connected? What if her aunt was signalling the Highwayman with the lantern? That would be an important reason to keep it a secret.

Could it be? Was it possible? Wouldn't it be delicious!

Kathryn picked up the pace. She was on her way to see a lady who may be able to supply some answers.

OPENING HER DOOR, Madame Ducharme took one look at the fish and her face lit up with delight. *"Merci, ma belle petite fille."* Then she caught herself and switched to English. "Thank you, my granddaughter."

"Aunt Belle thought you might enjoy these for dinner."

The old woman eyed them appreciatively. "It's been a while since I had any rainbow trout and I will remember you both in my prayers tonight. Will you come in for tea?"

Instead of her usual reaction to the offer, Kathryn had been hoping for an invitation. She had a mystery to solve. Was her aunt up to something clandestine and did it in involve the Highwayman?

She was sure Madame Ducharme knew everything that went on in River Falls and would be able to help shed some light on the lantern mystery. She almost giggled at her clever pun, then noticed the old lady waiting expectantly. "Oh, yes please," she said hastily. "To tea. It's been a long day."

"Wonderful. I'll put the kettle on while you clean them."

"Clean them? The fish?" Kathryn asked bewildered. They'd been sloshing around in a dish pan for the last twenty minutes, surely they were clean enough?

"There's a knife on that stump." Kokum indicated a well-worn chopping block not far from her back door.

It was then that the full horror struck Kathryn. "You want me to...to *gut* the fish?" Thinking of the deer she had seen being dressed, her stomach roiled at the prospect. "No, no I can't possibly do that," she stammered. "I mean, I don't know how."

"Then it's high time you learned. Cut open the belly and scoop out the innards. *Très facile!*"

Kathryn gulped as she carried the bowl to the stump. She picked up the knife and felt beads of sweat spring out on her forehead. "I will not let two dead fish defeat me!" she growled, trying to bolster her confidence while calming her stomach. "For King and country!" Taking a deep breath, she plunged the knife into the first fish.

It was the most disgusting thing she'd ever had to do. Swallowing bile with every breath, Kathryn managed to remove most of the entrails, the beasts' slimy fishiness making them difficult to hold and giving the Lilliputian sea serpents an odd animation as thought they were still alive.

How was she ever going to get the odour off her hands, and... She quickly checked her dress. What if she'd accidentally smeared some of the offal on her clothes? She'd smell like a fishmonger forever.

Taking the mutilated remains back into the cabin, she placed them in the sink and gratefully sat for her hard earned tea. She hoped the ordeal would be worth the answers she got.

"Madame, I mean Kokum, isn't it wonderful how the Highwayman knows exactly which transgression to right and when someone needs help or even special, rare medicine? I wonder how he gets this information..."

The elder offered Kathryn a cookie. "He travels so much, I'm sure that he hears many things."

Kathryn reached for one, but when she brought it to her mouth, the lingering smell on her hand made her place the pastry back on her saucer. "The thing is it happens so swiftly. Perhaps he is in contact with someone in River Falls and they tell him whom he should help next."

Madame Ducharme hesitated, her cup halfway to her lips, but not a flicker on that wrinkled countenance gave a hint as to what the matriarch was thinking.

"Perhaps God sends an angel to tell him what he needs to know. Or he may receive a blazing sign that he is needed." Kokum took a long draught of her tea.

Kathryn put her own cup down. An angel, not likely; a blazing sign, perhaps.

"And if I had a particularly nasty problem, how could I be sure the Highwayman would hear about it?" she asked innocently.

Kokum's attention focussed on the sink as she eyed the

fish hungrily. "What's that, dear? Oh, you don't have to worry. He'd know about your troubles immediately."

Kathryn wondered what that was supposed to mean.

The elder rose and hobbled to the stove. "I think you should stay and have supper with me, since you cleaned those fish so well."

This unexpected invitation caught Kathryn by surprise. "Thank you, but I couldn't. Aunt Belle is expecting me home."

"We shall send a message to her that you will be dining with me." She shuffled to the door where an iron triangle hung on the outside of the cabin. No sooner had the elder struck the gong, than a familiar face appeared in the doorway.

"You rang, Kokum?" JP asked; then, spying Kathryn, he removed his signature hat and winked.

"Yes, scamp, go to Belle's and tell her Kathryn shall dine with me tonight."

"Your wish is my command." And in a twinkling, he was gone as quickly as he had appeared.

Despite the grim beginnings, the fish meal turned out to be delicious and Kathryn thoroughly enjoyed her trout. The sun was well down when she bid the grandmotherly woman good night.

"Come back soon, my dear!" Madame Ducharme called as Kathryn started down the dark road for home, the wash basin tucked under her arm.

As Kathryn made her way through the dense pines near her aunt's cabin, a noise made her stop. She strained to listen, every rustle in the brush making her blood rush a little faster. The marauding bear was never far from her thoughts. Then she heard it. The sound of horse's hooves coming from the direction of Aunt Belle's and it was getting closer.

The thick clouds in the night sky made a mockery of the moon's brilliant light. Still, she hastily moved back into the deeper shadows and hid behind a tree, some instinct warning her it was best not to be seen.

In a cloud of powder-fine dust, a horse and rider sped past her. She saw a man dressed in black astride the dark horse, his hat pulled down low over his brow. Yet, even in the gloom, it was possible to make out the black mask and the flash of ivory at his waist.

It was the Highwayman!

Before she could react, the apparition disappeared into the darkness, leaving Kathryn breathless and shaking. He was real! And he was exactly as she'd pictured him – tall, muscular, fearless...mystery personified!

There was something else. He was dangerous. Kathryn ran for the cabin as fast as her wobbling legs could carry her. Cutting through the woods to avoid the road in case the rider returned, she stumbled several times, tripping and falling, but at last Kathryn burst through the door, gasping. "Aunt Belle! Aunt Belle! The Highwayman, I saw him!"

Her aunt, clutching a large bundle of fabric in her

arms, stood speechless for a moment before reacting. *"Mon Dieu!* Let me put this material away, and you can tell me all about it." She struggled up the steep stairs with the bulky textile; then returned, her face rather flushed.

"Now, where did you see this phantom rider?" She asked, leading Kathryn to the small horsehair settee.

"On the road, not far from here. He wasn't a phantom; he was real! Didn't you hear him? He had to pass right by the cabin." She was trembling all over. She'd actually seen him. Her Robin Hood had stepped out of her imagination and into the real world.

"Are you sure it was the Highwayman?"

"Yes, yes, he was masked and on a tall black horse." Kathryn was still shaking.

Her aunt put a comforting arm around her. "What an experience for you. Did he see you, *ma chère?*"

Kathryn shook her head. "No, I don't think so. I had stepped off the road and was hiding in the woods. I'm sure it was him." She took a deep, steadying breath.

"Well, that was an adventure." Aunt Belle patted Kathryn on the knee. "And how was your dinner with Kokum?"

Belle couldn't believe that her aunt was being so cavalier about this terrifying incident. "Aunt Belle – I don't think you understand the gravity of my experience. I saw the Highwayman of River Falls!"

"Yes, Katydid. You saw the Highwayman, the friend to all the Métis people. There was nothing to fear. You sit while

I get you a warm cocoa and you can tell me everything."

This was not the response Kathryn had expected. Thinking about it, she supposed her aunt was right. He was not your typical outlaw – he did *good* deeds. Never in all the tales she'd heard of this man had there been one incidence of violence.

As they sipped their drinks, Kathryn feeling calm once more, told her aunt all that had happened, including having to clean the disgusting, if delicious, fish, at which Aunt Belle laughed heartily. It had been quite the day and by the time the cups were cleared, Kathryn was more than ready for bed. She tried to stay awake to watch for the red light again, but was asleep seconds after her head touched the pillow.

THE NEXT MORNING, Katherine couldn't believe what she found on the cabin steps. She'd been on her way to give Nellie breakfast and when she'd stepped out the door they'd been there, waiting for her like friends come to call.

Books! Beautiful, wonderful, marvellous books.

"Aunt Belle, come quickly! Wait till you see what's here." Kathryn picked one volume up and then another. It was like finding a buried treasure on a desert isle. She was Jim Hawkins and she'd found a prize more valuable than Long John Silver's gold.

"What is it, dear?" her aunt asked, coming onto the porch.

"These books," Kathryn excitedly held up two, "these are the exact titles I need to continue my studies. That list I wrote out when we went to the Carter Academy, they're all here, with a few extras that sound very interesting!" She was practically giddy with excitement.

"My, my, where could they have come from?" her aunt exclaimed.

She said this with a straight face, but Kathryn thought she detected something in her tone. "I think we both know the answer to this riddle. Why, the Highwayman, of course!" She scanned titles and flipped pages as she shook her head, puzzled. "How did he know?"

Kathryn stopped mid-flip. The Highwayman must have somehow found the paper with the listed titles. Had her missive accidentally been thrown away only to be blown into his Sherwood Forest? Or – and this was a definite possibility – had the rogue broken into the cabin when they were away and stolen it?

Claude Remy jumped into her mind, black hair, dark horse and all. The day she'd tested him, he'd certainly made himself at home, barging right into the cabin without an invitation, not commenting on the new room – as though he'd seen the renovations before.

"Aunt Belle, where's that paper with the names of the books I needed?"

Her aunt thought for a moment. "In the china cabinet where I put it for safe-keeping."

Kathryn hurried back into the cabin determined to see for herself. She was sure she'd find the list missing, proving that Claude Remy, also now known to her as the Highwayman, had indeed been snooping around.

Opening the glass-paned door on the cabinet, Kathryn was flabbergasted to see the list, folded neatly and stuck in a small porcelain vase. "I don't understand.... How could he have known?" She waited for her aunt to explain.

"Well, don't fault me, Katydid! It's exactly where I put it."

This had to be another Métis miracle – courtesy of the Bandit de Grand Chemin. The problem was Kathryn couldn't accuse anyone, least of all the mad woodsman, without proof.

Chapter 12

UNCLE TOM'S CABIN IN CANADA

"Katy!" Her aunt called as Kathryn sat in her room leafing through the newly arrived books. "I have to go to town. Would you like to come?"

Kathryn debated internally: stay, and continue to peruse her latest treasures, or visit the *big city?* Shopping was most tempting, even in a less than metropolitan centre like Hopeful, and she could continue getting acquainted with her new friends when she returned. Plus, the idea of another thrilling carriage ride was irresistible and she didn't care what excuse was needed. Flying across the country-side in the Phaeton was one of the few things she would miss about living in this wasteland. She'd never done anything like that back in Toronto.

Slamming the book shut, she jumped off the bed and darted into the main area of the cabin. "The answer is *oui,* of course!"

Belle pulled off her apron and hung it in the cupboard. "When I delivered her dresses to the barracks, Mrs. Prentiss had left a letter ordering three new outfits for her daughters and a full-length sheared beaver coat for her.

The girls' dresses are complete; now I need the trimmings for the coat."

At this, her aunt became very animated. Kathryn couldn't understand why any one would get excited about taking on a mountain of such eye-straining, finger-blistering work.

Bustling about the cabin, Aunt Belle continued to explain the new project. "I had this idea to fashion a detachable hood for the coat. It would make it very versatile. Left on, the hood would give extra warmth against the cold. Remove the hood, and the coat would become much dressier and appropriate for mass on Sunday and fancy parties. It will be fabulous and very chic."

Kathryn wouldn't argue on that point, mostly because she didn't care. "Can we take the usual transportation?" She gave her aunt a Cheshire cat smile.

"Of course! And there may even be time to visit the Apothecary Shop for a licorice stick. It's a weakness of mine."

Kathryn made a face. "I must admit to having several sweet tooths – or is it sweet teeth? – and wouldn't mind some tasty confection. But not licorice – I detest the stuff. One lick and I have the worst digestive distress you can imagine." The dreadful root upset her stomach so badly she would have to take a long walk, alone, until it passed.

THE RIDE WAS EXHILARATING. Then Aunt Belle shocked Kathryn by handing over the reins.

"You may have to take the buggy one day when I'm not around, so you'd better know how to drive it."

"Back home, ladies don't drive carriages. We hire men to do that sort of chore." Kathryn shied away from the proffered reins.

"Out here, we don't hire people, Katy; we're the people folks hire. Surely you understand that by now."

Accepting the challenge, Kathryn tried gingerly shaking the reins: the merest suggestion to Nellie that it would be nice if the old dear could amble slowly, cautiously into town, no rush, they had all the time in the world; then with what Kathryn could only describe as a completely evil sounding whinny, the crazy horse raced off as though the hounds of hell were snapping at her tail.

Controlling the beast quickly proved to be quite beyond Kathryn's abilities. They hit a deep rut, causing the buggy to come perilously close to tipping. She shrieked, yanking on the reins as Nellie ran off the road and detoured into the tall grass. Pulling hard, she managed to get both the horse and the buggy back on the road where the Phaeton slewed dangerously back and forth, so violently that Aunt Belle finally had to retake the reins to prevent a total disaster, much to Kathryn's relief.

The experience was terrifying and Kathryn wanted nothing more to do with driving the Phaeton, or any other conveyance. One had to know one's strengths and being a mule skinner for a particularly stubborn jackass was not hers.

Nellie, contrary beast that she was, knew immediately who was in control and docilely complied with anything Aunt Belle requested without balking, biting or running wild. By the time they tied up the horse in a shaded alley in town, both Aunt Belle and Kathryn were laughing again.

"Would you deliver these to Sergeant Prentiss at the barracks while I pick up a few provisions?" Her aunt gave Kathryn the bundle of dresses.

"Of course. I'll meet you back here in a tick." Kathryn knew that building well as it came with the fondest of memories. It was where she had first laid eyes on her new suitor, Mark.

When she entered the detachment, a big man with a clay pipe clamped between his teeth was pinning up a poster on the wall. His brown field jacket was impeccable and the buttons polished to a gleam. The lanyard running down his barrel chest was spotless and Kathryn's eye was drawn to the well-worn gun holster on his belt.

"Excuse me; do you know where I can find Sergeant Prentiss?"

He turned to her. "You found him, ma'am." It was then Kathryn noticed the four chevrons on his sleeve.

"Belle Tourond sent me to deliver these dresses. Where

would you like them?"

"My wife's been expecting those." The sergeant gave his head a shake as the corner of his mouth opposite the pipe, twitched up into a smile. "There's a church social on Sunday and she wants her little girls to outshine all the other little girls. Doesn't seem very Christian to me, but after fifteen years of marriage, I've learned not to argue with my commanding officer. You can put them in the storage room in the back."

He indicated a hallway at the rear of the office.

In the passage, Kathryn found two unmarked doors, one on each side, and further along, barring her way, she saw another labelled *Cells*. Curious, she tiptoed down the hall and opened this one a crack. The three cells were cold and sparse, each with a wooden sleeping platform and a chamber pot. Horrid! There was also an exit to the outside and she wondered if it was through that grave portal that they led the condemned men to the gallows tree. It was a gruesome thought and she hastily returned to the hallway. Wondering which unmarked door was the storage room, she tossed a mental gold doubloon – after all, if one was going to use an imaginary coin, it may as well be a valuable piece – and chose.

Inside there was a chair and slung over the back was the slovenly brown uniform jacket she remembered seeing on Cyrus Blake. What a difference from Sergeant Prentiss's spit-and-polish regalia. This had to be Constable Dung's office.

The desk was strewn with papers and folders. She sniffed and winced at the fetid odour. There were stubbed-out cigars, empty bean cans, discarded and mouldy food, any or all of which could be the cause of the stink. How could anyone breathe, let alone work in there? Disgusting.

Trying the door on the opposite side of the hall, Kathryn discovered it was indeed the storage room with labelled boxes of files, rifles locked in a cabinet and a saddle on a wooden sawhorse with a tin of dubbin sitting beside it. Next to this, in a glass fronted cabinet, was Sergeant Prentiss's dress uniform. The red serge jacket blazed scarlet fire while the shiny spurs sparked like quicksilver on the highly polished knee high boots. Suppressing the urge to snoop into the other items in the cabinet, she wiped the dust off a crate and carefully laid the dresses down.

Closing the door as she left, Kathryn turned and ran full force into Constable Blake.

He leered rudely. "What are you doing here? Did you miss me?"

She stepped back quickly as though this time, she truly had met the Big Bad Wolf with his fangs bared and his breath reeking of rotten meat.

"I'm delivering a dress order for my aunt," she stammered.

"Belle's with you?" Blake asked eagerly.

"Yes, she's waiting for me now, and I'd better not be late." And with that, Kathryn edged by him, fleeing from the jail. That man was truly unsettling.

When Kathryn joined Aunt Belle, she didn't mention her encounter with the constable. She knew it would only upset her aunt. Instead, they discussed the new sewing project, or more accurately, Aunt Belle discussed the project as sewing was another of those domestic things Kathryn had no expertise or interest in.

As they made their way down the boardwalk, a group of whiskered men in severe black suits came out of a building. The party were talking amongst themselves as Kathryn watched them approach. Instead of parting for the two ladies, as all gentlemen should, the men seemed oblivious to Kathryn and her aunt.

"I hope Mr. McGraw got in his new shipment of buttons at the mercantile..." Her aunt stepped down off the boardwalk and onto the dirt street, narrowly avoiding dragging the hem of her dress through some fresh horse droppings. Without a pause, she reached up and pulled Kathryn after her. "I'd like something special for the beaver coat."

The men walked past with no form of acknowledgment or greeting, secure in their position as kings of the realm.

Once they'd moved on, Belle climbed back onto the walkway without comment and continued their conversation. "Of course, fancy will cost more but in my opinion, it will be worth it. If this coat is a success, other ladies will order from me and we'll be in the furrier business."

Kathryn was aghast. She stood rooted to the spot, gaping up at her aunt from the dusty street. "Aunt Belle!

Those, those...*gentleman!* Why did you make us step off the boardwalk?"

Her aunt's excitement of a moment before evaporated. "Katy, we don't want to cause any problems, and it's expected for us, for the Métis, to give way to those who live in town."

"You mean to the *white people.* That's utter nonsense. Unacceptable. I deserve the respect that should be shown any lady, no matter what her race. Scurrying into the gutter! Impossible!" Kathryn was furious as she climbed back onto the boardwalk and shook the dirt from her skirt. "When I read *Uncle Tom's Cabin*, I was so thankful I lived in Canada where cruel treatment of another human being because of his skin colour didn't happen. I see now, the sequel to Mrs. Stowe's novel could easily be written right here in Hopeful!"

"I don't like it any more than you do, Katy, but we have to live here. This is life for the Road Allowance People. Accept it." Without another word, her aunt turned and walked away.

Kathryn was stunned. Was this how it was for the Ditch People? They would forever be considered outcasts with every one going along like it was the right thing to do? She thought of all the Métis and the years stretching ahead. How would they bear it?

Silently, she followed her aunt into the mercantile, still dumbfounded by what she'd experienced outside. The most shocking thing had been that no one had thought anything of it. It was business as usual: white men on the boardwalk; Métis in the dirt.

The injustice of what had happened made the future lawyer in her seethe. Kathryn felt anger, shame, hurt and helplessness all at the same time. Toronto and her privileged life seemed very far away.

Aunt Belle took forever to choose the right threads, buttons, needles and other assorted frippery, checking each item a thousand times until she was satisfied.

"There, that should do it. I hope Mr. McGraw will let me put all this on my bill until I'm paid for the work. I don't have any money right now and there must be over five dollars worth of goods here." She held up her basket of loot.

They went to the counter so that Aunt Belle could arrange credit, but before she could say anything, a large woman with a garish purple dress and matching hat decorated with drooping bunches of fat grapes approached.

The woman gawked at Aunt Belle in her faded yellow dress, moccasins and braids, and her expression turned to one of intense disgust. It reminded Kathryn of the last time she'd stepped in something that was best scraped off her shoe. The rotund woman pushed in front of Aunt Belle and placed her own purchases on the counter.

After the boardwalk incident, Kathryn couldn't believe this was happening. Fury flashed white hot as her spine straightened. "Oh, no you don't. I believe we are next, madam." She firmly slid the intruder's basket aside.

"Well, I never!" The woman squawked indignantly, her face blossoming into the same purple shade as her hideous dress. "You sort are getting way above yourselves. You should be run out of town back to where you belong." Huffing loudly, she turned to the merchant who was at a loss as to what he should do. "Mr. McGraw, you should restrict the clientele you allow into your establishment. The City Ladies League all agree, these half-breeds should be barred from stores where decent people shop."

Kathryn's temper shot off the scale. "Why you..." She took a menacing step forward, about to really get into it when her aunt laid a silencing hand on her arm.

"Katy, please, it's all right, I'll wait. I have to speak to the proprietor about the details." She gave Kathryn a pleading look.

"No, it is absolutely *not* all right!" Then Kathryn realised she shouldn't cause any more trouble. Without those supplies Aunt Belle couldn't sew and that would mean no money to buy food. Reluctantly she gave in, biting back the scathing retort waiting to leap off the tip of her tongue. "I'll be at the chemist's."

Using every fibre of self control, she left the store before she turned the huge purple grape into a vat of quivering jelly.

CHAPTER 13

TRUTH LIES AND LICORICE

The bell over the door to the Apothecary Shop jangled violently as Kathryn stormed in. She grumbled scathing retorts to herself as she surveyed the orderly store for the penny candy display case. Taking her time, she inspected the rows of sweet treats, and finally, the tempting confections worked their magic. Her anger eased, and she marvelled at what any girl knowledgeable in the best delicious delights would have to rate as a first class selection.

She'd brought a small amount of coin with her, remnants from her train ride which seemed a million years ago now. As she searched the jars of available treats it occurred to her that she might not be served. A quick peek at her reflection in a wall mirror and she realised there would be no problem. Her smartly styled navy and white dress, in an expensive fabric, bespoke upper class. Plus her pale complexion and blonde hair, gathered at the nape with the grosgrain ribbon her aunt had given her, assured that she did indeed, look a young lady of acceptable lineage.

Spotting the pharmacist, Kathryn cleared her throat politely. "Excuse me, sir."

The proprietor dropped his pestle into a salve he was compounding. "What can I do for you, miss?"

"How much are your licorice sticks?"

"Penny each. It's a *penny* candy counter."

His tone was friendly and Kathryn relaxed. "May I ask why you have a candy counter in a chemist's shop?"

He walked over to the display and pulled a piece of the vile root her aunt loved out of its jar, offering it to her. "Why, everyone knows a little sugar is the best medicine for most ills. I haven't seen you before. Is your family new to town?"

Kathryn thought of what had happened in the mercantile. "Yes. We live..." She motioned vaguely in an unknown direction. "Over there."

At that moment, the bell tinkled again and Kathryn turned, expecting her aunt, instead, she was captured by mesmerizing grey eyes.

"Hello again, Just Plain Kathryn."

"Good afternoon, Mark. How nice to see you." She touched a strand of hair that had come loose while she'd been doing her raging.

"Here for a sweet treat?" He nodded at the licorice stick she held.

"Actually, this is for..." Kathryn hesitated, and then opted for the easy way out. "Yes, yes, that's right. It's mine."

Mark reached into his vest pocket. "Please allow me." He flipped the pharmacist a bright copper penny.

"Why, thank you. How gallant." Elated, Kathryn giggled. She'd never been bought candy before and even though it was technically for Aunt Belle, she would record receiving this piece of loathsome confection as a life first.

"Not that you need any sweetening up," he added.

Mark shuffled his feet and Kathryn took this as another very good sign. He was as nervous as she.

"Well, go ahead..."

"Go ahead...?" She smiled coyly, hoping to hide her confusion.

"Go ahead and have a chew. Don't wait on ceremony with me. I know how much you ladies like your candy."

Kathryn's smile faded as her stomach gurgled. Mark continued to wait expectantly. She suppressed a shudder and tentatively nibbled on the end of the dried root. "Mmmmm."

He watched her with pleasure.

Kathryn continued to gnaw on the tough twig, saliva pooling in her mouth as she felt her gorge rise and her lower regions rumble. What was it about this accursed stuff that made her body react so violently?

The cause didn't matter; the effect did. She had to leave, before something unforgettable happened, something of the mortifying type of unforgettable.

"I'd love to stay and chat, regretfully I must dash. I hope to see you again soon." Holding up the disgusting stick, she forced another fractured smile. "And thank you for this. It's so...yummy," she lied brightly. Turning, she fled the store.

Once safely outside, Kathryn breathed a sigh of relief as she spit into the dirt, trying to rid her mouth of the obnoxious taste. She'd had enough of Hopeful's excitement for one day and decided to wait for her aunt at the Phaeton.

Walking down the boardwalk, she spied Aunt Belle across the street also on her way back to Nellie and the buggy. Kathryn was about to call out when, as her aunt entered the alley, she abruptly stopped.

Squinting, Kathryn wondered what the problem was and then she saw him. There in the shadows, Constable Cyrus Blake stood with his horse, waiting. He was like a nasty troll hiding under a bridge.

Fearful, Kathryn hurriedly crossed the rutted road toward what she knew would turn into a bad altercation. She rushed down the wooden walk but before she could make it to the lane, Kathryn caught sight of Mark exiting the apothecary's. She certainly didn't want him coming to her assistance. She felt terrible as the true reason for this became clear.

Kathryn didn't want to have to explain why she was defending a road allowance woman. She pretended to examine the hats in a milliner's window, praying Mark would not come over to continue their visit. With relief, she followed his reflection in the glass as he walked away in the opposite direction.

Apprehension made her heart beat faster as Kathryn

willed herself forward, toward the alley and the shrouded shadows where at this very second, her aunt could be in terrible peril, but she found she couldn't move. Fear of what was waiting and, she shivered, *who* was waiting with her aunt had turned her feet to stone.

There was also something else; something she didn't want to acknowledge and Kathryn pushed it from her mind.

Her imagination painted a dire picture of Aunt Belle facing down that thug alone. Kathryn put herself in the same situation, cornered and in need of help, then forced herself onward. The earth spun slower on its axis and her steps crawled though she knew every second counted.

Constable Blake's back was to Kathryn as she stepped into the gloom. Pausing, she listened to what was transpiring between her aunt and the troll. It was not going well and she desperately wished some daring champion would materialise right now. The Highwayman immediately came to mind and she glanced over her shoulder, but the sunny street was deserted. No masked salvation would be riding in on a dark horse.

"You must have a lot of time on your hands out there alone in the woods. I could mosey by and keep you company. I know where you live..." Blake's tone was insinuating and insulting. "And now that you have that pretty little girl living with you, it would be worth my while to pay you both a visit, kinda two for the price of one."

Kathryn held her breath. She knew her aunt used good

common sense and infinite patience in her dealings with the citizenry of Hopeful; however, Blake and his outrageous disrespect coupled with the unmistakable threats to both of them was something else entirely.

Heart thumping, Kathryn took a hesitant step deeper into the alley. Blake's hulking form made a tempting target and she wished she had a weapon. A large gun perhaps, but her hands were shaking so badly, maybe a stout club where aim wasn't such a big factor would be better.

Belle's voice was strong when she answered. "I get along fine, especially now that Claude Remy is back from his trap lines. You remember Claude. He's a big man with the short temper."

Blake laughed out loud. "I'm not worried about that buck."

He moved closer and from her vantage point, Kathryn saw her aunt forced further into the alley, a stack of large wooden crates blocking the scene from watchful eyes. Finally, Aunt Belle was backed against the wall, literally.

Blake stretched out his arms, pressing the bricks on either side of Aunt Belle and blocking any escape.

"Maybe we should get better acquainted right now and I can meet your niece later."

Kathryn didn't know what to do. Paralyzed, she wondered if anyone would actually help her if she called out or would they think another half-breed was simply getting what she deserved.

At that second, Aunt Belle slipped under the arm of the constable and out of his grasp. She reached into a small paper bag; then, as fast as lightning, she pulled her fist out, stepped forward, and blew a black dust into the muzzle of Blake's horse.

Immediately, the animal sneezed, reared up on its hind legs and whinnied loudly. Blake grabbed for the reins. Straining, he struggled to stay on his feet as the horse pulled and bucked violently.

A large man brushed past Kathryn, running to help the constable.

"What's going on here, Cyrus?" Sergeant Prentiss demanded.

"Nothin,' Sergeant. My horse don't like the smell of this half-breed is all."

The sergeant's voice was like flint. "Then I suggest you take your finicky horse someplace else. You're late for work and my supper's waiting. Better get to it."

Relief freeing her, Kathryn hurried after the Sergeant. She felt sick at not coming to Aunt Belle's rescue. And what if it had been the other way around? Kathryn could never imagine Belle Tourond being afraid to help anyone in trouble. "Are you hurt?" she asked in a small voice.

Aunt Belle shook her head, smiling tremulously. "I'll be fine, thanks to Sergeant Prentiss."

"I'm sorry about this, Belle. Cyrus is a mite hotheaded," the sergeant explained.

"Cyrus is an idiot!" Belle retorted, stiffening her spine and standing tall.

Yet Kathryn could see that her aunt was slightly unsteady on her feet. "Aunt Belle, we should go home and have a hot cup of tea."

Her aunt gratefully agreed. "I think that sounds wonderful."

"This is your niece, Belle? I wondered who was delivering those dresses, but this young lady raced out of the barracks before I had a chance to ask." Sergeant Prentiss looked puzzled. "I didn't realize you had any kin."

"My brother from down east, he passed away recently and his daughter Kathryn has come to live with me."

The sergeant tipped his Stetson at Kathryn. "Welcome to Hopeful, miss. Your aunt is one fine seamstress. My wife's got a mighty long list of frocks she'll be ordering from Belle so I expect you'll be making more deliveries in the future." He straightened. "And speaking of work, I'd best get back and make sure my constable's there. Again, I apologise for Cyrus' behaviour." He touched the brim of his hat. "Ladies."

THE LATE AFTERNOON RIDE BACK to River Falls was a quiet one. Ripples of shimmering heat rose from the hot prairie and the air had a wonderful warm grass smell that Kathryn was beginning to find quite intoxicating. Her aunt, stoic as ever, sat tall and proud as she drove the little Phaeton home; even Nellie sensed something was amiss and was on her best behaviour.

As she stared at the passing fields, Kathryn went over and over the encounter with Blake. She refused to think of what the nasty brute might have done to her aunt. How terrible to have to worry about being attacked by the very person charged with protecting you! It outraged Kathryn but in the light of her new understanding of the Métis situation, she knew it was futile. Some Clara Brett Barton she was. Defender of the weak? Advocate for the helpless? Hardly! The first time she was put to the test, she had failed – and failed spectacularly.

It was then Kathryn remembered the other troubling thought that had slowed her steps and she cringed at the memory. The stark truth was she simply hadn't been able to face more grinding abuse of any kind. The dreadful session with the bigoted tyrant at the Carter Academy, then the incident on the boardwalk with the arrogant city fathers and the infuriating session with the ignorant purple prune in the mercantile had drained her to the point of breaking. Given the chance, she'd happily shove a few of these ignorant peasants into the castle moat.

It had also made her understand why her father had to get away from this. It was impossible to rise above the water if your head was always being held under.

How did the other Road Allowance Métis deal with

this day after day and stay so happy? They did indeed need a champion.

And at that instant, the Highwayman, who ever he may be, became Kathryn's biggest hero, her noblest knight and staunchest defender of the less fortunate. He was more than all those put together and she cheered his exploits. The Highwayman was a hero in the truest sense of the word!

BY THE TIME THEY ARRIVED HOME, Kathryn was exhausted from the stress and couldn't imagine how her aunt felt. While Aunt Belle prepared their tea, Kathryn started the fire. She watched as the hungry flames devoured the wood. It was mesmerizing and she stared blankly into their fiery depths, the day's events swirling in the embers.

"Katy, you're very quiet. Are you feeling ill?" Her aunt asked as she placed the tea tray down.

Startled out of her reverie, Kathryn was about to say she was fine, then without warning, something shattered inside her. "I do feel sick, Aunt Belle, but it's not what you think." She rubbed her forehead, squeezing her eyes shut. "This afternoon...I, well, I..." She didn't know how to say the words, then, facing her aunt, the shame rushed out. "I was there, I saw what Blake was trying to do to you and I froze. I was afraid and did nothing. I feel sick that I was such a coward."

"Oh, *ma chère*, don't blame yourself. Of course, you were

afraid. What happened today was terrifying."

Her aunt reached out for Kathryn's hand but she pulled it back. "No! No excuses. My behaviour was despicable. I should have been rescuing you and instead, I abandoned you. I am a terrible person. Oh, Aunt Belle, I am so dreadfully sorry. I will never abandon you or anyone else in need again. I promise with all my heart if only you will forgive me."

The pain in her aunt's eyes was almost too much to bear. Kathryn felt her knees start to shake. Surely Aunt Belle must hate her, but the words that came next, made Kathryn want to sing with relief.

"You are not a coward and you are most certainly not a terrible person." Aunt Belle sadly shook her head. "Today was overwhelming Katy, and you have already been through so much. Blake is a rabid dog and no one in their right mind would go near an animal like him. I am a grown woman who has faced abuse for many years and I was afraid! Don't chide yourself for an honest and normal reaction. There is nothing to forgive. We are home and we are both safe. I love you, dear one, and will always love you."

Kathryn rushed to her aunt and Belle's arms folded protectively around her, warm and comforting. They held each other for a long while, then her aunt kissed the top of her head.

"Come, Katydid, you promised me tea."

With a much lighter heart, Kathryn poured the hot, black beverage and listened as her aunt extolled the virtues of the exquisite buttons, perfect thread and other wonderful bits and bobs she had purchased today.

Finally, as evening crept stealthily in, they sat together enjoying each other's silent company, the only sound the ticking of the mantle clock and the occasional crackle as the logs burned down to ash.

"It was really quite a day, one you'll remember, I'm sure." Her aunt said at last.

"Definitely not one I'd like to repeat," Katherine sighed, tucking her feet under her as she curled up in the comfortable wing chair. She remembered Aunt Belle mentioning Claude Remy, almost as though threatening the constable with her jealous, tough boyfriend. Unfortunately, Constable Blake hadn't been the least bit worried about the big woodsman, which was short-sighted on his part. Having an angry suitor the size of an ox hunting you for harassing his fair lady was not something any right-minded interloper should take lightly.

It reminded her of Madame Ducharme's story about Belle's fiancé, Gabriel. Her aunt wasn't unattractive, nor was she really that old. Kathryn wondered if her aunt was lonely having taken on the role of the Spinster of River Falls.

"Aunt Belle, may I ask you a rather personal question?"

Her aunt seemed not the least taken aback. "Of course.... But there is no guarantee I will answer it." A ghost of a smile played on her lips.

"I was wondering if you're lonely, living here in your

cabin in the woods."

Belle paused and her face took on a soft expression. "I won't lie to you. I miss my Gabe. He is the best man I ever met and I cherish every minute with him. We have a destiny together."

Kathryn noted Aunt Belle's manner when speaking of her departed beau. She was obviously unwilling to face the fact that he was dead. Sometimes, we keep our loved ones so alive in our hearts that we refuse to let them go. It was tragic and Kathryn ached for her aunt but she understood especially when she thought of her father. "He sounds like he was a wonderful man."

Her aunt poured the last of the tea. "How about you? Did you leave a special someone behind in Toronto?"

Kathryn blushed. "Me? Oh, no, the convent wasn't exactly overrun with suitable young men and when we did have a social, the 'black crows' were ever vigil so that none of our reputations were sullied. What this meant for we young ladies was that there was never a chance to learn more from the young men than their names."

Picking up her cup, Kathryn's face filled with mischief. "Aunt Belle, I have to know. What did you throw at the horse?"

Her aunt sipped delicately. "While at the store, I bought a little black pepper since we're running low and thought I'd share it."

Her aunt stated this so matter-of-factly, Kathryn was

unsure she'd heard correctly. Carefully, she set her cup down and cleared her throat. "Apparently, Aunt Belle, horses don't like pepper, any more than I like this..." She withdrew the licorice stick she'd tucked in her pocket before the trouble started.

Belle's face lit up as though Kathryn held an enchanted bean that would grow a stalk to a castle in the clouds. "Oh, Katydid! You clever girl. Thank you."

She reached for the treat, only to have Kathryn hold it out of reach. "I have to warn you. It's slightly used."

"I don't care if Cyrus Blake licked it..." Aunt Belle stopped. "No, wait, even for a licorice stick, I can't stoop that low! Darn close though. Now, hand it over." She made a lunge for Kathryn and both of them dissolved into laughter.

Chapter 14

OUTHOUSE RENDEZVOUS

Over the following days, Kathryn kept busy helping her aunt clean the house, wash the clothes, feed old Nellie, tend the vegetables in the large garden and do a host of other domestic drudgery. How Aunt Belle did all these household chores and was a seamstress as well, Kathryn didn't know. By nightfall each day, she was exhausted and wanted nothing more than to have a hot bath and fall into bed to read more of Sir Giles's daring exploits.

Kathryn had also been having less than restful sleeps. She tossed and turned all night, strange dreams jolting her awake as cold sweat soaked her nightdress. Many of these dreams were of her father. Always, he would slip from her grasp, ephemeral as the colours of a rainbow, and try as she might, Kathryn couldn't hold him. She would greet the day irritated and out of sorts.

It was after one of these nightmares that Kathryn awoke with a start. A noise from the main room roused her and then she saw it. Seeping under the gap at the bottom of her door was the strange red light she'd seen before. Jumping out of bed, Kathryn scurried to the bedroom door and yanked it open.

Her aunt, standing at the table, whirled and clutched her chest. *"Mon Dieu,* child! You scared me half to death."

"Oh, I'm sorry. I saw the light..." She took in the lantern glowing on the table, glowing with a perfectly normal yellow light, and then scanned the room. It was the only lantern there.

"Oui, my child. I don't go out at night without a lantern. Too many visitors prowling around who don't like to be startled. You never know how they'll react."

"No, it's the lantern. The light was red. " Kathryn protested, the whine in her voice verging on childish.

"Well, as you can see, there is only this one and it's a plain, ordinary light, not some fairy lantern. Now, off to bed."

Then Kathryn saw something peeking out of the pocket on her aunt's coat. It was a tiny piece of gauzy material and it was a rich, ruby red.

Kathryn shuffled back to her tiny room. Wide awake now, she sat on the edge of her narrow bed. The walls she had whitewashed herself glowed iridescently in the moonlight, the reflection casting an eerily bright light.

Why was her aunt avoiding telling the truth unless she was up to something she wanted to keep secret – and what was the biggest secret in River Falls?

The Highwayman.

The two had to be connected. Kathryn loved

mysteries and there were enough here to keep her busy for a month of Sundays.

Then she remembered the day she and Mark had shared lunch by the river and they'd seen Aunt Belle racing to who-knew-where. Kathryn thought of how well her aunt had sat her horse. Even Mark had been impressed.

Out of the blue, a phrase from Sister Bernadette's vernacular popped into Kathryn's head. She had been guilty of *a sin of omission* – when she'd compiled her list of possible suspects, she had not even considered the Highwayman could be a woman.

This added many more suspects to her list, but Kathryn couldn't deny the possibility. A bandanna could cover a face, and long hair could be tucked up under a hat. Take her aunt, for example: she was strong, could ride like the wind, plus she lived alone and apart from the rest of River Falls. Kathryn recalled the night she'd seen the Highwayman. How foolish she had been to cut through the woods – the road would have been faster, and she might have caught her aunt stashing the evidence and returning to the cabin...

Kathryn shook her head. Aunt Belle the Highwayman? Impossible! Agitated, she paced the room. Some dime-novel detective she was. She was surrounded by mysteries and had yet to solve one satisfactorily.

Out of all her suspects, who was most likely to be this unknown hero? She concentrated, trying to think like a lawyer and immediately, Claude Remy again headed her list. Most of the identifying marks fit, if you used your imagination a little for the details. She thought of Claude's visit when she'd tried to discover if he was the Highwayman. What had been his final words?

"Tell Belle I have the goods."

The goods! Reaching out, Kathryn stroked her fingers down the spines of the beautiful volumes. Could he have been talking about books – a load of very hard to come by and exactly what she needed books?

She felt her heart speed up a beat or two as a string of events linked themselves together like pearls in a necklace.

The night of the dance, Aunt Belle had said Claude had stayed behind. What if he'd slipped away to do good deeds and everyone thought he was walking them home? And he was a trapper, who came and went for long periods and at odd times. Then there was the way Claude had strolled into the cabin like he owned the place, as though he and Belle had an understanding that this was acceptable.

What if Aunt Belle was using the red lantern to signal Claude Remy – to tell him about some problem at River Falls that needed fixing? A midnight rendezvous would be a great way of relaying the needs of the people without attracting attention, especially if Belle pretended not to like Claude to confuse the gossips even more. Circles within circles. It was the perfect smoke screen.

Those circles whirling in her head spun faster and faster.

It made sense. The Highwayman needed an insider to feed him information, one who wouldn't be suspected of sympathizing and who lived in a remote area which made meeting with her secret red signal *tres* easy.

No wonder Kokum has said the Highwayman would know about her troubles immediately. Kathryn was living with the telegraph operator!

It all made sense. She jumped back into her warm bed. She'd done it! She'd positively, absolutely unravelled the mystery of the unknown Highwayman, and given him a name – Claude Remy. This was so exciting: diversion and danger; mystery and mayhem; and, to make it completely intriguing, Romeos and romance. She really was a dime-novel detective!

Kathryn had stumbled on the Métis Robin Hood and his beautiful Maid Marian all in one swoop!

THE NEXT DAY, Kathryn was humming to herself as she swept the cabin floor. She hadn't decided what to do with her revelation and would have to carefully pick her moment when she told Aunt Belle that the jig was up.

"That's enough housework, Katy." Her aunt motioned out the window. "Why not escape and enjoy the sunshine for a while."

Aunt Belle was busily pinning the hem of the dress she was working on. Even hanging from the dressmaker's dummy, Kathryn could already see how elegant it would be when finished. "I could use some fresh air."

"It's a wonderful day. You should take advantage of our river and go cool off."

Kathryn considered this. "That's a great idea." She picked up the book she was reading, eager to get to the good part, and grabbed her straw bonnet from the coat peg at the door. "See you later."

Ambling down to the river, Kathryn felt the heat of the early summer sun through her cotton blouse. It was going to be a scorcher later on and she was glad she'd remembered her hat. The sun brought out the freckles on her pale face and she detested them. They made her look like a child.

At the riverbank, she picked the perfect spot for wading, shucked her shiny patent leather shoes and itchy stockings and, hiking up her skirt to a shocking inch above her knee, sloshed into the cool stream.

The rocks were slimy with glistening green moss and small black minnows darted away in the sun-dappled water. The air was fresh and smelled so sweet it made her want to inhale until her lungs burst.

As Kathryn played in the stream, she unexpectedly felt an urgent need arise. All that water, splashing water, swirling water...

She clambered onto the bank and, for fear of wetting her lovely leather shoes, walked barefoot back through the pines to the privy.

No sooner had she sat down, when a branch snapped loudly outside. She paused, listening. "It's occupied, Aunt Belle."

Instead of her aunt's normal reply, all Kathryn heard was a sort of deep grunt, then a snort. The hairs on the back of her neck stood up. That was not how her aunt usually sounded.

"Aunt Belle? Is that you?" Her voice quavered.

There was now a distinct scratching sound at the flimsy wooden door. Something was outside! The clawing moved higher up the wood.

Did bears feed in the day time? Did bears use outhouses? Then there was a loud thump and a bang on the back of the rickety building.

Kathryn shrieked and made the sign of the cross. Shaking, she leapt up and put her eye to a crack in the door, expecting to see a thousand-pound grizzly with eight inch claws and ten inch teeth waiting for her to come to dinner where she'd be the honoured guest and the main course!

She couldn't see anything. Should she run? Was it safer to wait until the beast grew bored and left? Should she play dead? How long would it be before she wasn't playing?

When the small building started to rock, Kathryn knew she had no choice. Taking a deep breath, she burst out of the door and ran for the stream, remembering too late that grizzlies hunted salmon in rivers and it was a nice day for paddling.

The sound of raucous laughter made her stop. She turned to see JP doubled over with hysterics.

"You should see your face!" he howled, clutching his sides.

Kathryn felt the heat in her cheeks. "You rat, JP! Come here and we'll see how my fist looks in *your* face!" She dashed after him, determined to drown him like a rodent in a gunny sack!

He ran behind a large pine, dodging her flailing fists as he deftly leapt onto a log that extended into the river. Not about to be foiled, Kathryn rushed forward, hoping to send the annoying boy flying into the stream.

She miscalculated her momentum, and too late realized she couldn't stop. The impact sent them both arcing gracefully, even artfully, into the frigid water.

The shock made her gasp. "I can't breathe!" she squeaked.

He slapped her on the back, a little too hard she thought, which freed her paralysed lungs and she sucked in a huge lungful of air.

Struggling with her soggy skirt, Kathryn dragged herself out of the water and sat with a squish. "You idiot! What were you thinking? You scare me half to death and then you try to drown me!"

JP retrieved his bright red hat from the safety of the

branch where he'd stowed it and placed it on his head. "For the record, it was *you* who tried to drown me." He adjusted his chapeau a quarter inch to the left. "Thinking about it, I guess I did need a bath." Satisfied, he came to sit beside her.

"What are you doing here, anyway?" She shook her blouse to release the water, acutely aware of the way it clung to her and caused the chemise underneath to be seen plainly through the now transparent white cotton.

"I came to borrow the promised book. If I remember rightly, that was part of our deal." There was a challenge in his eye.

"And you couldn't have come to the door like a normal human being?" She squeezed her braid, draining more water.

"I did! Didn't you hear me scratching?" He was positively gleeful.

This was too much. Kathryn pulled back her fist and socked him on the arm — hard.

"Ow!" He grabbed his shoulder. "That's my old war wound. Bit of shrapnel from the Crimea."

She snorted. "You're holding up well for your age."

They sat in mutual silence until pitiful won out and Kathryn relented. "Fine, truce. You can have the book." There was a detail from a while ago that still bothered her and this annoying boy may be able to help. "JP, you once told me you knew things about all your subjects, is that true?"

"Verily, I say unto you, I know enough to get more than one of our fine citizens in some rather hot water."

She pursed her lips. "Can you tell me, if a man keeps his knife on his left side, is he right- or left-handed?"

JP jumped to his feet, brandishing a stout branch. "If one must deal with evil foes, one should carry a sword and be prepared to use it at a moment's notice. If one is right handed, he would carry his blade thus..." He slid the tree limb into his belt on the left side.

Claude had had his knife on the *right* side – so he *was* left handed! She clapped her hands, sensing victory.

"But..." JP paused for effect. "If one carries a knife, one carries it on the side one is most adept with. If you are wrong-handed, you carry it on the left, which always leads to frustration as knives and their sheaths are set up for right-handed folks, which most are."

This was not what she wanted to hear. This would mean Claude was right-handed...unless it was a ruse. Had Claude deliberately worn his knife on the opposite side to throw pursuers off with misinformation? That would be very devious and clever, and though she could believe Claude was devious, it was a stretch to consider him clever.

"And now, fair maiden, about my book..."

She came back from her wool gathering. "JP, it's *my* book; don't forget that I need it back." It was going with her when she left. "But I think a knight of your renown can be trusted. Come on, I'll show you what I have."

They walked, joking and teasing each other, back to the cabin, where Aunt Belle was now busily hammering inside Nellie's lean-to.

"She's making a coop for April, May and June," Kathryn said excitedly.

JP's face was a study in bewilderment.

"We have three new chickens and I named them so we could keep track of who was whom," she explained.

He dusted his wonderful hat, then replacing it, tipped the brim to a jaunty angle. "So will you eat them in order of the months they were named after?"

Kathryn took a swat at him which he easily avoided. "They'll be 'egg only' fowl, thank you very much."

After she'd changed out of her damp clothes, they spent the next hour discussing the merits of each book, until finally, her visitor chose the very one Kathryn was going to read next. It was on her 'Personal Favourite List' and considering what was going on in River Falls at the moment, she had thought to re-read it to refresh her memory on heroes of yore.

"I might have known." She gave him her copy of *The Merry Adventures of Robin Hood of Great Renown in Nottinghamshire.*

JP hefted the large volume. "This should keep me going for a while. It weighs a ton!"

"The weight is not important, it's the content." Kathryn sniffed derisively.

He opened the book to the last page. "With 987 pages, it's *heavy* on content!" He continued to eye her other books greedily. "And can I have that one next?" He indicated her cherished copy of *Ivanhoe*.

This one she wouldn't part with. It had been the last book her father had given her and she'd been saving it, waiting until the time was right. She had yet to start and wanted to be the first to read it. "Let's see how you do with the one you have."

Kathryn watched as JP left, waving and laughing as he swept her a gallant bow before disappearing into the trees. She wondered how long it would take him to finish a book the size of *The Merry Adventures of Robin Hood*. Surely, long enough that she would have the money for her train fare home which meant she'd have to retrieve the book before she left.

She'd been giving it thought, and wondered if she could get a position as a clerk in a store for a short period; or perhaps, Aunt Belle could teach her some sewing tricks. Unfortunately, any of these ideas required extremely long hours for very little pay. The prospect of staying over the winter was terrifying. There was no way she would be here for Christmas. Maybe she should say a prayer to Saint Jude, the patron saint of lost causes.

For the rest of the day, Kathryn wondered and worried on how she would come up with the money she'd need. There didn't seem to be a solution and by the time they'd finished supper, she had a pounding headache.

"What's wrong, Katydid?" Aunt Belle asked concerned.

"My head is throbbing. Maybe I'll turn in early." She really did feel awful.

"I have just the thing. You get ready for bed and I'll bring you something that will help."

Kathryn retired to her room and when her aunt came in with a bitter tasting draught, she made a face.

"It will help you sleep," her aunt explained.

Kathryn couldn't argue and downed the entire glass. Moments later, her eyelids felt so heavy, she blew out her light and fell into a deep sleep.

THE NEXT MORNING, Kathryn was startled to see JP running up the path towards the cabin. Surely, he hadn't read that book in one night! Now, that would be a mighty feat fit for a knight of the realm.

"I must speak to your aunt immediately." JP said breathlessly.

"She's still working on the hen pen." Kathryn could tell by his face that something was terribly wrong.

They found Aunt Belle in the shed busily nailing down the last of the chicken wire.

"Have you heard the news, Mademoiselle Belle?" JP asked as soon as her aunt put down the hammer.

Belle pulled off her work gloves. "What news?"

"Kokum sent me to deliver this." The young man removed his hat then withdrew a piece of paper tucked inside. "Last night, the bank was robbed and the guard stabbed and killed. Blake and Edward Meltzer, he's the murdered man, were guarding a payroll for the Crowsnest Coal Mine, over seventy thousand dollars, when they were attacked. It was the biggest payroll the bank had ever had." JP took a deep breath before going on. "Blake says it was the Highwayman and he's organized a posse to hunt him down."

Aunt Belle read the notice. "This is not true! Murderer? Bank robber? All lies! What proof do they have?"

"Everyone knows the *Bandit de Grand Chemin* carries a knife with a fancy ivory hilt. It was that knife that killed the guard. Constable Dung says he wrestled it away from the Highwayman before he was knocked out." JP shook his head.

Kathryn took the paper from her aunt and read it. It was a wanted poster, like they used to put up in the wild west back when Wyatt Earp and Billy the Kid roamed the range.

$5,000 Reward
Paid for the capture of the
Murderer and Bank Robber
known as
The Highwayman
DEAD OR ALIVE
Union Bank, Hopeful, Alberta

Dead or Alive! Kathryn re-read the notice. Could they

do this? Was this legal, even out here in no man's land?

"Kokum said she truly hopes the Highwayman knows that he's being hunted and that he's gone to ground and stays hidden." JP smoothed the raven feather on his hat. "Do you have any message for her?"

"Tell her..." Aunt Belle shot a quick look at Kathryn. "Tell her I'll come by for tea later." Without another word, she gathered her tools and returned to the cabin.

"She's very upset." Kathryn watched her aunt retreat.

"Everyone in River Falls knows The Highwayman is no murderer, nor did he rob the bank, and they'll swear to it. That won't stop the white man from hanging him for it anyway. He's convenient and with that price on his head, he won't last long." The disgust in JP's voice was unmistakable.

"That is a lot of money and they have the knife." Kathryn was mesmerized by the paper with all those zeros.

"Trumped-up evidence. There are lots of knives with ivory grips around." JP was defiant even though they both knew this wasn't true. He struck the side of the shed with his fist. "This makes me so angry. We can't fight the white man. Constable Dung loves a good funeral, and this one's going to top his list."

"If he's a constable, then he's supposed to arrest the suspects so they can have a fair trial." Kathryn protested.

JP scoffed. "It depends on what colour your skin is. The whites want to stop anyone who helps the Road Allowance

People. The bankers and fine city fathers, who complain our Highwayman is a thorn in their sides, now have him pegged for murder and robbery – and Dung has provided them with the evidence to justify the rope. Plus they're dangling a fortune in reward money."

Kathryn had to think. "None of this makes sense, JP. Why would the Highwayman commit murder? Every other time he's pulled off a..." she didn't want to say *crime*, "transgression, he went out of his way not to use violence. Now, he does this terrible thing knowing he'd be hunted forever. How can he continue to help the Métis if he's running from the law? It would be like poking a hornet's nest. And the knife – if the Highwayman knocked out Constable Dung, why would he leave it behind?" She paced up and down. "And isn't it a bit convenient that Cyrus Blake is the only witness left since the poor guard ended up dead? The Highwayman guilty...impossible! Aunt Belle will have to warn him tonight."

JP raised his brows. *"Your aunt will have to warn him tonight?"*

Kathryn realized she'd let slip a detail better kept to herself. Fortunately, JP was not about to run to the authorities with any information that would help capture the Highwayman. He could be a valuable ally if she took him into her confidence.

"JP, I believe Aunt Belle is in contact with the Highwayman. I've seen her leave the cabin at night with a red-shrouded lantern and the next day, some injustice against the Métis has mysteriously been righted. I can't think it's a coincidence."

"Talk like that could be dangerous, *mon amie.*"

Kathryn lifted her chin. "I'm not afraid of Constable Dung."

"I didn't mean for you." JP made a subtle hand movement indicating the cabin. "You should *fermes ta bouche* about such things."

It may have been meant as a warning, but it sure sounded like an insult to her. He was so infuriating. "I must go to my aunt." She left the lean-to without another word.

As she hurried to the cabin, her mind kept replaying the same thing:

$5,000.00...

$5,000.00...

FIVE THOUSAND DOLLARS!

With that kind of money, she could go back to Toronto, finish her schooling and go on to university. Becoming a lawyer would magically change from a dream into reality. This was fairy godmother territory.

What was she thinking? There was no way she could ever do something so traitorous. But if she could be swayed so easily by the promise of that gigantic reward, imagine how many people, maybe even in River Falls, would be happy to turn in the Highwayman.

She could easily see how someone as rough and ready

as Claude Remy could rob a bank, especially a white man's bank, with no problem. She knew how he felt about whites. Was he capable of murder? Yes. He could do it, but *would* he do it, that was the question. This went way beyond filching a couple of cans of paint or a few books. If he had done something so wrong, so revolting, then he deserved to go to jail. The law was the law.

Chapter 15

SURPRISE FIRST

After seeing to Aunt Belle, Kathryn went to sit on the side of the hill above the river to figure things out. Was the Highwayman, hero to the Métis and mystery man of legend, a bank robber and murderer?

All the wonderful deeds she'd heard attributed to him would lead her to say – *impossible!* He only bent the law to ensure that justice was done for the Métis who were being treated as second- or even third-class citizens. Right?

And didn't the fact that Claude Remy had little problem bending the law of the land show that he had no scruples when it came to disobeying the rules? And wasn't he strange and a little scary in the first place? And didn't everything on her list overwhelmingly point to him being the Highwayman?

But being the Highwayman didn't automatically mean he was guilty of the robbery too.

All this dithering was dismissed when she considered the biggest, most important part of this puzzle. Constable Dung. If ever there was a skunk that stunk, it was Cyrus Blake.

The death of the guard was tragic and also very convenient for Blake. A little bell went off in her head. What if he'd driven off the robber and then decided to take the money for himself? Or perhaps there'd been no one else involved at all.

What if Cyrus Blake had killed the guard, stolen and hidden the money, then put the blame on the Highwayman? That sounded more likely. Blake, she was sure, would have no trouble killing someone in cold blood. He'd done it to Gabriel Ducharme. If she were a betting sort of young lady, she'd put money on that bigot being the guilty party in all this mess.

The lawyer in her addressed the court. *What about the evidence, m'lord? Consider the knife, the very distinctive, carved-antler knife.* That was the fly in the ointment. It was proof Claude had been at the scene of the crime. She had to find out if he still had his knife and if he didn't, should she turn him in?

Kathryn thought again of the five thousand dollars. No one wanted to see an innocent man go to jail for something he didn't do. On the other hand, a guilty man should receive the full weight of the law and if she helped, shouldn't she be rewarded?

If Claude didn't have that knife, was that proof enough for her to turn him in and collect the reward? Could she sleep at night if she did?

Despite the warm sunshine, Kathryn shivered. She felt

miserable. She wanted her old life back, one where she knew what to do and if she didn't, she could ask her father, who always had the answers. Swiping at her stinging eyes, she focused on her predicament.

Kokum said she hoped the Highwayman knew he was being hunted and would take precautions. Kathryn was sure Aunt Belle would act tonight to ensure he was warned using the mysterious red lantern as the signal for a meeting.

Claude had disappeared and everyone assumed he'd gone back to his trap lines, or to that hidden cabin in the woods, but with the aid of that lantern, Kathryn was sure he would magically reappear tonight.

"Fancy stumbling over you here, Just Plain Kathryn."

Kathryn jumped, then lifting her head, sneezed as the bright sun dazzled her, sending swirling black dots across her field of vision. She shaded her eyes and saw Mark towering above her. "Oh, it's you." Her tone was dismal.

"You really know how to make a fella feel welcome." He sat beside her and picked a long piece of prairie grass, sticking it between his teeth.

"I guess that was a little rude, I'm sorry. I have a lot on my mind." She didn't know what to say, she didn't know what to do. One thing she did know – having Mark here was the best thing that had happened all day.

"When I got grief, I found the best way to deal with it is to get some whiskey and forget my worries."

Kathryn was appalled. "You drink whisky? You're only

seventeen!" His face told her she'd said the wrong thing and was relegated to the category of idiot – again. "I mean, no, I think I'll pass."

Mark spit the stalk out. "Hey, I heard something interesting from a friend of mine. He said Alberta is really going to be put on the map this summer. The first steam car is coming this way. A gent by the name of Billy Cochrane has this Locomobile he's driving around and he's coming to Calgary. That little beauty develops twelve horse power and can reach the unbelievable speed of forty miles-per-hour! Imagine it. That's the vehicle for me."

"I thought you wanted a Phaeton." Kathryn decided the fickleness of young men was astounding and, more irritating than that, why wasn't he more sympathetic about her problems?

"That buggy is a mighty fine ride until you put it up against a horseless carriage. Woo wee! That's the way of the future, girl."

His enthusiasm was mind boggling and again, irritating. Kathryn drew her legs up and tucked her skirt tight around them, the chill still lingering from the cool grass. She rested her head on her knees. "I don't feel like talking about horseless carriages."

"You really are out of sorts. Maybe I can help."

He moved closer and put his arm around her. Kathryn's head flew up. She tried to control any further reaction, wanting him to think she was a woman of the world and used to gentlemen embracing her. He tightened his hold and she could practically feel the iron in his arms. No boy had ever had his arm around her before. She wasn't counting wrestling with JP because he was such a child.

Then without warning, Mark leaned over and kissed her...*on the lips!*

If he hadn't been holding her so tightly, Kathryn was sure she would have floated up into the clouds. The word *swoon* danced in her brain and she understood how a lady could actually faint from the thrill of such a momentous event. She settled closer into his encircling arm basking in the afterglow and sighed contentedly.

Her first kiss – that meant something. His affection was obvious. Kathryn thought of all her terrible troubles. Maybe she should share her burden with Mark. After all, he was older, with the wisdom that came with age and he was so strong and...*he had kissed her.* Surely, she could trust him now? And it would be such a blessing to share her burden. She made a decision. "I have a problem. If I tell you, I need you to promise to keep it our secret. It must remain between us."

"I won't say a word, honest injun." He promised.

Kathryn winced at the trite reference. Perhaps this wasn't a good idea after all. She didn't want Aunt Belle or the River Falls people to be limelighted, but then she looked into his eyes, limpid pools she could dive into.

To be honest, Mark's eyes were actually more limp than

limpid – a dull shade of gray like a cloudy January sky – and yet, she still felt like jumping into their fathomless depths.

"It's about the bank robbery. I saw the poster for the capture of the Highwayman. I've heard how he helps people and I think that's wonderful and brave, but if he's a murderer and a thief, then he should go to jail." Her shoulders slumped dejectedly and her buoyant mood sank. "I guess I don't want Robin Hood to turn out to have feet of clay."

"Feet of clay? That's not possible, even in the circus." Mark was incredulous.

Kathryn stopped; a little stunned at his words and then smiled indulgently. Her new beau was so charmingly naive about so many things. "No silly. *Feet of clay* is an expression that means he's not some special hero, helping the helpless, only an ordinary man like the rest of us – able to slip, to be human and, in his case, maybe rob a bank."

Mark squirmed uncomfortably. "That part about you being *an ordinary man like the rest of us,* that's another of your expressions, right. You ain't no guy?"

Disconcerted, Kathryn gave him her most indulgent womanly smile, this one perhaps a little more forced than the last. "Mark, dear heart, what I'm saying is that I admire the Highwayman for helping the Ditch People and I don't want him to be the guilty one." Pretending to be arranging her skirts better, she inched closer. "I don't believe he would do something so wrong. It doesn't make sense."

"How can you know anything about that desperado

and who are these *Ditch People?* Honestly, girl, sometimes you talk crazy and I can't make heads or tails out of it."

"You don't understand, Mark. I know who the Highwayman is."

He squinted down at her, disbelief written on his face. "You can't possibly know something like that. You only moved to town a few weeks ago and you probably don't have much to do with his kind."

Kathryn tried to qualify her statement. "Well, maybe not *know* know. I am pretty sure who he is, though, and if I can find him, I could see if he still has his knife which would refute the evidence Constable Dung has." She explained, thinking out loud.

"Constable Dung?"

He seemed to be having trouble keeping up with her train of thought, in fact, he sounded like he wasn't even standing on the platform! She tried again. "Cyrus Blake – that slimy, low down, no good, shifty, disgusting…"

"Whoa, there little filly. Constable Blake? He tried to save Ed and then fought the thief. Took his knife and got mashed up for his trouble. And to add insult to the whole thing, Cyrus was working on his day off to help guard that payroll."

"Oh, pul-ease! If this Highwayman was so blood-thirsty, why didn't he stab Blake too? No, there's more to this than the constable is telling. The good thing is that my aunt can contact the Highwayman. In fact, I think she'll arrange a meeting tonight and I'm going to be there to see if our Robin Hood still has that very special knife."

Mark tensed. "Your aunt can bring this outlaw in? Who's your aunt?"

"Belle Tourond. She uses this special red lantern to signal him and they meet in the forest somewhere..."

"A lantern? Where does she live that she can wander into the forest to meet this criminal?"

Kathryn didn't know why he was asking her all these ridiculous questions. What he should be asking was if she wanted him to come with her tonight, to protect her from wild beasts and if she would permit him to kiss her goodnight later.

"We live in River Falls, well, actually, away from the area where most of the houses are, closer to the river in the cutest little log cabin."

"She's one of those road allowance squatters! That's who you're calling Ditch People?" His eyebrows shot up. "You said you came from Toronto. That means you're a, a..."

She was getting impatient with him now. "Yes, yes, I'm an *Easterner* who knows nothing about woodsy things, but Aunt Belle is teaching me." The afternoon sun made a halo of his brown hair and she thought he was an Adonis. Kathryn smiled at him and she knew her heart was easily read in that smile. She didn't care. Mark was a wee bit trying, true. He was also funny and strong and so handsome.

"Gotta go."

With a quick movement he stood and as Mark was now her official beau, sealed with a kiss, she waited for him to help her up. Instead, he sashayed back down the hill without so much as a by-your-leave.

Kathryn clambered to her feet and ran to catch him. "I'll see you again soon?"

Mark stuck his fists into his pockets of his dungarees, appearing she thought, very, *very* sweet, like her very own Tom Sawyer, except Mark always smelled vaguely of a pig barn.

"You bet. I'm countin' on it."

She watched him walk away, the tall grass swishing against his pant legs as the sun silhouetted his long, lean body and it was only after he'd left that she realised he hadn't actually said he'd come with her tonight.

Chapter 16

NIGHT LIGHT FIGHT

The sun slipped behind the tall pines and as the long evening shadows drew in, Kathryn prepared for the night ahead. She still wasn't sure exactly what she was going to do should this midnight rendezvous between her aunt and Claude take place. Would she stand bravely and accuse him of being a low-life bank robber and murderer, or say she believed Constable Dung was using him for the scapegoat and manufacturing evidence? It would depend on one critical detail – if he had that knife.

Aunt Belle was sitting by the fire when Kathryn came into the cabin. She moved to the warmth of the hearth near her aunt. "The fire is an excellent idea."

Her aunt's voice was weary. "There's *li rababoo di naryi-aanl* for supper," she corrected herself, "moose stew, and I've made some bannock and fetched fresh milk from the well. Shall we eat?"

This was so like Aunt Belle. Her world was certainly not bright right now; still, she had enough strength to take care of her little Katydid.

Kathryn stopped – taken aback. She had referred to

herself as *Katydid!* She must have had too much sun today.

"Thank you, Aunt Belle. The milk sounds like the drink for me, but I bet you'd rather have a cup of tea."

Her aunt sighed, *"Oui, merci."*

There was no wood for the stove, so Kathryn went outside, deftly split two lengths and hurried back to stoke the fire before putting the kettle on. As she pushed an extra piece into the firebox, she congratulated herself on chopping the wood into exactly the right size to fit.

Kathryn bustled about putting dinner on the table. She wanted to show her support for her aunt helping the Highwayman, which was hard to do when she wasn't supposed to know what was going on. Perhaps if she casually mentioned something positive, it would cheer Aunt Belle.

"I am sure the Highwayman is far from here and safe." She lied with a smile. "And any Métis in the world would gladly help him evade the constable until the real murderer can be found."

She hoped this was true, trying not to think of the reward money herself. "I think the Highwayman is a real hero, don't you? Very Robin-Hoodish." She took another large spoonful of the spicy stew which tasted delicious.

"Yes, yes he is," he aunt nodded in agreement, "and much needed. Until the Métis people are treated as equals and with respect, we will always need someone to balance the scales."

Kathryn knew she had to couch her words carefully. "I truly hope he knows about Blake and that posse JP said he'd rounded up. It would be terrible if he walked into a trap."

"*Oui.* I will light a candle for our Bandit de Grand Chemin."

Or a lantern, Kathryn thought.

Kathryn retired for bed as early as possible hoping to give her aunt plenty of time to prepare for the rendezvous. So much had happened today and if she was right, it wasn't over yet.

Snuggling down under the covers with her book propped up on her knees, she thought of her afternoon with Mark. He may not always be the brightest firefly in the jar, but he was certainly attractive enough to have stepped out of a fairytale. And the kiss...

She sighed and, making a fist, tried to re-enact the momentous event, gently pressing her lips to the faux mouth the side of her hand made. It wasn't the same at all – there was no spark, no electricity, no *je ne sais quoi...* Some things were better real than imagined.

She wiggled, adjusting the layers she had on. Under her nightdress, she was fully clothed, which would allow her to be much faster when she followed her aunt later.

Not wanting Aunt Belle to think anything was amiss, Kathryn decided to finish the chapter she was reading before turning out the light and pretending to sleep. She'd left the door open a tiny crack which would alert her immediately when the red lantern was lit. Everything was working out perfectly.

There was a knock, and then her aunt peered round the door. "I'm heading to bed and thought I'd see if you needed anything before I turn in."

Kathryn yanked the covers up a little higher, in case her strangely bulky body alerted her aunt. "Oh, I'm fine."

Aunt Belle smiled warmly. "Good night, Katydid."

Hours later, Kathryn was focusing on staying awake and finding it more and more difficult. She paced in her dark room, listening. All was quiet in the cabin, and it occurred to her that there was a slim chance she'd been wrong about all this; that Aunt Belle would not go to warn the Highwayman. After all, her entire scenario was built on pretty flimsy evidence – a midnight trip to the latrine and a brief glimpse of some red cloth. Her aunt was a seamstress - perhaps the cloth had simply been a material sample for some ladies new gown? She hadn't thought of that until now. Had she made a giant mistake?

A rustling from the main room made her stop. She listened and sure enough, there was the sound of someone moving about. With a smile at her own cleverness, more like brilliance, Kathryn silently moved to her bedroom door and peeked out the crack. It was Aunt Belle and she was...

She was putting more wood on the fire and wasn't wearing her coat, nor was she carrying a blasted lantern.

Impossible! Kathryn yawned sleepily, longing to dive into her comfy bed, with the fluffy duvet and the puffy pillows with the lovely embroidered cases.... No, she couldn't let her thoughts wander off the path. She had a mystery to solve and perhaps, a hero to save.

Watching her aunt, she saw her return to the ladder leading to the loft, and climb the steep steps. This was not working out the way she'd anticipated. Perhaps her aunt wouldn't go until tomorrow night, if she went at all. Kathryn was about to jump into bed, when movement on the stairs caught her eye. Aunt Belle was coming back down.

Kathryn held her breath. Her aunt, now dressed and wrapped in her shawl, carried a lantern as she moved to the table where she struck a match to light the lamp. Pulling the red cloth out of her pocket, Aunt Belle covered the lantern, flooding the room with a crimson glow; then she moved stealthily to the door and silently disappeared into the night.

At last! She'd been right! This was Kathryn's cue. Triumphantly tearing off her nightdress, she swirled a cape around her shoulders and fled after her aunt.

The night was lit by the all-seeing full moon, the brilliant white orb providing the light she'd need to trail Aunt Belle to the secret assignation. Several times, Kathryn could have sworn she saw someone hiding in the woods, but upon closer inspection, these phantoms turned out to be gnarled branches or clumps of willows. In the distance, the wavering red glow bobbed through the darkness, a reassuring beacon.

Ahead, a small glade opened and it was here that her aunt stopped, placing the red-shielded lantern on a large boulder.

Using the trees and bushes as cover, Kathryn tried to get as close as possible without being seen. A fallen log, lichen covered and shrouded by ferns, provided the perfect hiding spot to wait for the meeting. She lay behind the tree sinking into a soft bed of moss that cradled her like some sweet smelling byre.

The sound of snapping branches jerked Kathryn awake. She'd fallen asleep! How long had she been dozing? She listened to the noises of the night and heard a rider approaching. Peering over the top of her fallen log hideout, Kathryn waited for the arrival of the elusive hero.

His horse was indeed as dark as midnight. She squinted – in fact, it was black. When the Highwayman swung down from the saddle and took Aunt Belle in his arms, Kathryn could have positively melted. In his dark outfit and black mask, he appeared extremely handsome and mysterious, even if she knew in the daylight, as in Cinderella, her hero would turn back into a lumpy pumpkin called Claude Remy.

As she watched, the couple exchanged a soft kiss, her hero gently touching Aunt Belle's cheek in such a tender gesture that Kathryn could have fainted. It really was Robin Hood and Maid Marian.

Claude appeared more athletic in his Highwayman guise, a phenomenon Kathryn attributed to the odd light cast from the red lantern and the brilliant white moon.

It was this wonderful moonlight that allowed her to

see the knife on his belt. It was there – on his left hip, the ivory handle glowed a phosphorescent white. Kathryn's heart leapt. He still had his knife! It was the proof she needed. The Highwayman, the hero of the Métis people, was not a despicable criminal.

It was then that another noise caught Kathryn's attention. She listened more closely and realized it was the sound of horses approaching, a lot of horses, and they were coming fast. Did the Métis Robin Hood have a band of Merry Men as had the legendary do-gooder of yore?

None of her stories of the Highwayman mentioned anything about accomplices. Something was terribly wrong.

At that moment, she spied a group of mounted men galloping toward the glade where her aunt and her hero were unaware of what was coming. Kathryn's breath caught in her chest. There could be only one explanation. It must be Blake and his posse!

Aunt Belle and the Highwayman were about to be caught! Kathryn jumped to her feet and raced toward the two unsuspecting lovers. She burst into the glade and picking up the lantern, dashed it to the ground, extinguishing the red signal light.

"It's a trap! You have to run!"

Her warning came too late as, in a cloud of dust and thundering hooves, the troop of riders charged into the clearing.

Dread gripped Kathryn when she spied the leader. His hat drooped to one side. It was Constable Blake and he had a gun aimed directly at the Highwayman. Kathryn screamed as a shot rang out. Pandemonium ensued. The horses' reared and bucked, terrified, as men shouted. It was chaos.

At that moment, her aunt must also have recognised Blake. She picked up the broken lantern and swung it, smashing the constable square in the chest. He howled in rage, lunging his horse at Belle and knocking her to the ground.

Kathryn vainly tried to push the horse backward, only to stumble and fall in the dirt with her aunt. The posse surrounded the women and though Kathryn searched frantically about, she could see no trace of the Métis hero known as the Highwayman.

"You stupid little breed!" Constable Blake spat into the dirt at Kathryn's feet. "He escaped and it's your fault. I won't forget this." Then Blake turned his dead eyes on Aunt Belle. "The night's not a complete bust. We have you and I'd say since we missed our main target, you should hang instead. Everyone will agree you had to be in on the bank robbery, probably been hidin' that thieving, interfering buck all along."

Aunt Belle rose shakily to her feet, but when she spoke, her voice was steady. "You have me, let my niece go. She had nothing to do with this."

Blake sneered. "She's such a pretty little thing. Are you sure you want her staying *all alone* at that shack of yours, Belle? Could be, she'd come to some harm." He laughed and his men joined in, as though he'd said something extremely funny.

Kathryn stood, looking him straight in the eye. "I am fully capable of taking care of myself, Constable. Aunt Belle showed me how to shoot a gun in case any *vermin* show up." She prayed she sounded stronger than she felt.

This brought more derisive laughter. Then Blake reached down and yanked Belle by the hair, dragging her onto his horse with him. "I think you'll like the accommodations I have waitin' for you back at the detachment."

And with that, he spun his horse and the entourage disappeared into the night, with Aunt Belle kicking and fighting. There was a rider who hung back in the shadows, behind the rest, but before Kathryn could identify him, he too was swallowed by the darkness.

Kathryn sank to her knees, rocking back and forth. If she'd been a minute earlier.... If she'd shouted.... Her heart ached at the thought of Aunt Belle in that monster's clutches. This was a nightmare and she felt terrified as Blake's deadly threat rang in her ears. Could it happen? Would they hang Aunt Belle? In this savage land, anything was possible.

There was no sign of her hero. He had escaped – to where she could only guess. If she were the Highwayman, she'd hide until she could form a battle plan to get both him and Aunt Belle out of danger. The logical place Claude Remy would choose was that secret cabin of his. The problem was Kathryn had no idea where that was or how to find it.

Chapter 17

WHO FIGHTS THE BATTLE NOW

The sun was struggling over the horizon as Kathryn stumbled down the road toward Kokum's house. She needed help and the wise elder, as leader of the community, was the logical one to take charge. Kokum would have to gather all the people of River Falls then go save Aunt Belle from the hangman's noose. Kathryn knew there was strength in numbers.

Her mind flashed to her aunt languishing in that cell, completely at the mercy of that twisted constable and she shuddered. Something had to be done and quickly. She believed Blake's threat of hanging was real.

An article she'd read recently in one of Aunt Belle's newspapers crept into her brain. It had reported the execution of Black Jack Ketchum, a notorious member of the Hole in the Wall Gang, and how when they'd hanged him, something had gone wrong and he'd been decapitated. His head had been pulled right off his body. Kathryn's flesh crawled.

At the old woman's cabin, JP sat morosely tossing pebbles into the dirt. "Is Kokum here?" she asked anxiously.

"*Oui.* Inside." He answered without looking up.

Kathryn hesitated. JP appeared miserable to her, even the jaunty black feather in his hat hung loosely. Whatever the problem, she had no time for it now. Quickly moving past him to the door, she knocked, and then barged in. The elder was sitting in a chair near the window, embroidering.

"Kokum, something terrible has happened...." She went over the events of the night before. The frail old woman turned deathly white and Kathryn was afraid she was having a heart attack. "JP! Get Kokum some tea, *now!*" The authority in her voice must have alerted the young man to the urgency of the situation as he hurried into the cabin, saw the elder, and hastened to bring the healing draught.

When the hasty tea was finished, Kathryn continued. "Constable Blake is behind the bank robbery, I'm sure of it. The Highwayman is simply a convenient scapegoat. Now he's saying Aunt Belle was an accomplice. We must gather everyone and go to the barracks to save her."

Kokum slowly shook her head and Kathryn saw a hundred years of sadness written on her ancient face. "My child, that is not our way. If we interfere it will lead to more bloodshed. The white man will do what he wants and we cannot stop him. Demanding the impossible will only bring more trouble down on us."

Kathryn stared, speechless. This was not the response she had expected from the feisty elder. "Didn't you hear me? Blake threatened to hang Aunt Belle! *Hang her!* You are the leader of River Falls. If we stand together, we can be a voice that will be heard. They can't ignore all of us and we can demand a fair trial for Aunt Belle. We must do this, Kokum."

The old woman's resignation was something Kathryn could not and would not accept. She straightened, feeling older and more sure of herself than ever in her life. "I believe in the Rule of Law, for everyone. There shouldn't be one set of laws for the whites and another for us. I don't want to be treated as some sort of leper, shunned as though I were unclean. You docilely accept this terrible way of life as though it were normal. You live in tarpaper shacks that can be burned down at any moment; your children can barely read or write because they can't go to some ridiculous *whites only* school; you allow yourselves to be cheated and robbed, young girls attacked, all so you don't *bring more trouble down on yourselves!* Well, I've got news for you, Kokum. It's already here! And I for one am not willing to let those jackals tear Aunt Belle apart!"

Kathryn left without another word. She was furious. Kokum was the matriarch of this community, but when it came time to fight for one of their own, she turned into a feeble, weak old woman afraid to face the storm.

JP followed her outside, still moping as though he'd lost his best friend. "Oh, for heaven's sake, what's wrong with you?" Kathryn demanded.

"How could you do it, Kathryn?"

Something in his tone made her stop in her tracks. "What are you talking about? Do what?"

"I saw you yesterday, with Mark Prentiss. You were kissing him." He closed the distance between them. "Did you know Constable Dung is his uncle? Then last night, the Highwayman is almost caught in a trap, and you happened to be there. Isn't it lucky that you were the only Métis not arrested? Did you go to gloat when the hero of the *Ditch People* was taken down?" He'd worked himself into an angry lather.

Kathryn's mouth went dry. "Mark *Prentiss,* he's the sergeant's son?" What had she done? She'd told him all about the secret signal and that Aunt Belle was going to warn the Highwayman.

The rider who had hung back in the darkness, it had been Mark. She groaned. "Oh, no! This is all my fault. I told Mark about the signal because I thought he..." she faltered, "I thought he liked me. I trusted him."

Then she remembered how he'd reacted when she'd told him that Belle Tourond was her aunt. His sudden cool attitude and his parting words how he was counting on meeting her again soon. He must have run straight to his uncle and told him everything.

JP stepped closer. "You come here, upset everyone with your, your...*books*, then you cut the heart out of our community. Do you have any idea how much the Highwayman meant to every Métis? It wasn't simply the things he did to help our people; he was a symbol – one of hope, hope that we could change things, that it was possible to fight peaceably, without guns, and win. And now, thanks to you, that hope is gone."

His cheeks were wet with tears now, and this was somehow worse than the anger. He walked away, leaving her numb. It was true. She was at fault. She hadn't done it out of malice; no, it was way worse than that. She'd done it because she'd been foolish – utterly, recklessly foolish...over a boy.

And Kathryn realized that losing JP's friendship meant much more to her than losing Mark Prentiss. This Métis boy was a true friend, a friend you could laugh with, tease, and talk about books with, someone who cared about you. And now she'd lost him.

She thought of her papa. If her father had caused something as catastrophic as this mess, Kathryn knew he wouldn't lie down and accept defeat. Her father, who'd been so strong and brave, who had taught her justice and to stand up for what was right, he would wade valiantly into the fray.

But he was gone, forever, and so was her dear sweet mother. Gone, dead...a page turned in her mind, and she felt a hot tear squeeze out of the corner of her eye, then another.

It was as though a dam burst and she couldn't stop it. Kathryn let the tears fall and as they did, her grief fell from her also. Along with it, the hidden anger at her parents for leaving her was washed away until all that remained was a sense of peace and acceptance. She had been loved and Kathryn would always have that to carry in her heart.

She wiped her sleeve across her snotty nose. If it took a battle to make this right, then she'd give them one. She would fight for Aunt Belle, the one person who loved her unconditionally. Kathryn was a Tourond, and she wasn't going to give up so easily!

KATHRYN'S FATIGUE WAS BURNED AWAY by her anger. She raced for Aunt Belle's trying to come up with a plan as she went. The sun was up and that meant even tired constables would soon be at their work.

Taking the veranda stairs in one leap, Kathryn hurried inside the cabin and then stopped, trying to order her thoughts. What to do first? She looked down at her torn and dirty dress and the smallest of smiles appeared on her lips as she recalled her aunt's words from what seemed a lifetime ago. It seemed she again had on a frilly rig which wasn't practical for the task at hand. She needed something more suitable. Kathryn went to the ladder leading to the loft.

She'd never been in Aunt Belle's bedroom and immediately noticed the bed. The posts were four sturdy logs connected with wooden poles and rawhide interlacing formed the sleeping platform. On top of this was the mattress, if one could call it that – a canvas bag filled with fresh hay. Her quilt was made of patchwork unlike anything

Kathryn had ever seen before. It was tiny diamond shapes cut from many different hides of various colours and textures, sewn together in an intricate mosaic that was stunning. A true piece of art.

Kathryn thought of her own bed, with a real mattress and feather duvet, which if she were to be honest, was more comfortable than her bed back at school. Why had Aunt Belle given her the smart iron bedstead with the nice mattress and kept this crude canvas bag for herself? There was a lot about her aunt that she didn't understand.

Kathryn felt a little uncomfortable snooping through her aunt's wardrobe but she wanted the denim jeans and coat she'd seen Aunt Belle wearing while riding so skilfully.

If the good townsfolk of Hopeful wanted to treat the Métis as outcasts, then she'd act like one, right down to the clothes she wore. The blue jeans and capote were strange attire for a woman. They were also much more practical, not to mention more comfortable, than a long dress and shawl.

Once she'd changed, she ran for the stable to tackle her second challenge – saddling old Nellie. As she struggled with the bridle and other horsey gear, her mind ran over the events of last night remembering the fabulous knife she'd seen the Highwayman wearing. If Constable Dung had a knife as proof, it was a fake. Claude still had his fancy antler carved weapon in his possession.

Kathryn was now positive Blake was lying and the

reason had to be profit – seventy thousand dollars profit. The townspeople would want someone to pay and if two Ditch People were conveniently offered up, then silenced permanently, everyone would think justice was served and that the money had been buried in the bush, lost to the bankers. It would become part of the history of the town, then forgotten along with her aunt and the Highwayman. What a perfect plan!

So perfect, in fact, that Blake was sure to speed things up if he could.

She pulled on Nellie's cinch one last time, then buckled it. Clambering into the saddle on the large horse was no mean feat in itself but finally seated, Katherine set out to talk to each and every Métis family in the district. She would convince them that together they could do something remarkable- they could save Aunt Belle.

Kathryn's high spirits were soon tested as family after family said the same thing: they were barely scraping by now and they weren't about to cause more trouble. They were all very sad that Belle had been caught up in this, but they'd known the miraculous boon of the Highwayman couldn't last forever. Nothing good for the Métis ever lasted long.

By the time Kathryn finished her rounds, frustration had replaced her high spirits. The Métis had had years of hard lessons from life on the road allowances; still that was no excuse for abandoning Aunt Belle. She was one of their own and she needed them.

If it were left up to the Ditch People, her aunt would die. Kathryn had to stop that from happening by any means, fair or foul. She went over all she knew and kept coming back to one inescapable solution: Blake was the mastermind behind the robbery and murder, and it was up to Kathryn to set a trap for him before her aunt paid the price.

She needed to talk to Aunt Belle. With a nudge of her heels, Kathryn and Nellie started the long trip to Hopeful.

Chapter 18

DESPERATE PLAN TO
ESCAPE THE DUNGEON

Kathryn felt the hostile glares as she rode down the main street of Hopeful. It may have been because of the way she was dressed, but to use an expression she'd read in one of her dime novels, she *sat tall in her saddle* and defied the lot of them.

She suspected her clothes probably weren't the true reason for the hostility. It was more likely, word had gone around that the *new girl* was merely another Métis squatter from the road allowances and she was sure who had spread that word.

Tying Nellie up in the alley, Kathryn spied Mark Prentiss, her ex-suitor, tipped back in a chair as he lounged against the barracks. Fury bloomed as she strode across the street to confront him.

"You told Constable Blake about my aunt and her lantern signal, didn't you?"

He dropped the two front chair legs back down to the boardwalk with a bang. "I figure the likes of you road allowance trash get what you deserve."

His words stung like razor-edged slivers of ice. "Mark, I thought you and I, well, I thought you had feelings for me."

He stood, loathing coming off him in heated waves. "Get this straight. I don't have nothing to do with no red-skinned half breed."

Katherine's eyes glittered as she took a menacing step toward him. "You get *this* straight. You need to think for yourself. You've let the ignorance of others twist your mind. You liked me well enough when you thought I was white. Well, Mark, my skin is the same shade it was yesterday. The only colour to worry about here is the ugly one your prejudice has painted the world." She started past him, and then stopped. "And for the record, I wouldn't have you if you were the last pig farmer on earth!"

She slammed the door on the detachment office a little too hard as she entered. Sergeant Prentiss sat at his desk, frozen at her dramatic entrance.

"Whoa now, Kathryn! You need to know that's the only door I have and I'd appreciate it if you didn't rattle it off its hinges."

"Sergeant Prentiss," she rushed on. "My aunt had nothing to do with the robbery and more than that, the Highwayman didn't do it. Constable Blake said he took the knife away from the Highwayman and it was his proof of guilt, but that doesn't add up. If he was knocked out, why didn't the killer take the knife when he left or worse, stab

Blake like he did the guard Meltzer?"

The sergeant carefully set his fountain pen in the rest and replaced the lid on his small jar of ink before he spoke. "I know you don't want your aunt mixed up in this, and I'm thinking Belle was simply caught in the crossfire and is innocent. Cyrus has only been a member of the North West Mounted Police for two years and I'll admit, he's got a big mouth and he may be a might hot-headed. This Highwayman fellow of yours, he's a whole other story. He's been stealing from the townspeople for some time now. Nothing big, I know that, still...a thief is a thief. Maybe he decided taking all that money was the best way to rub our faces in it once and for all. I'm the first to admit there's been some unfair dealings and the Métis folks get the short end of the stick a lot, so I kind of turned a blind eye when the Highwayman started evening the score. The bank business is different. We're talking murder and stealing seventy thousand dollars. No one gets away with that, not if I can help it."

"What if I told you I had seen the Highwayman, and he still had his knife?"

The sergeant's face showed surprise at this, then immediately went hard. "You couldn't have, Kathryn. Cyrus has that knife put away for evidence."

"His knife is a fake. It has to be..." Kathryn knew this was not going well. Sergeant Prentiss had his mind made up.

"Why don't you go back and say hello to your aunt.

She'll want to see you." His voice softened as he indicated the narrow passageway which led to what she would call 'the dungeons'.

As she walked down the corridor, Kathryn passed the office she remembered belonged to Constable Blake. The door was open and the office empty. The same awful reek wafted out and she wrinkled her nose. Maybe Sergeant Prentiss kept the smelly fellow hidden from public view, which was what Kathryn would do if she had a snake like Blake working for her.

Hurrying down the hall, she pushed through the door to the cells and immediately spotted her aunt, sitting disconsolately on a wooden pallet which passed for the bed. Her braids were dishevelled and her soiled dress torn at the shoulder. The most shocking thing about her aunt's appearance was the dried blood at the corner of her mouth. Kathryn's stomach clenched as she rushed forward. "Thank goodness, you're all right!"

Belle stood and hurried to the cell bars when she saw who it was. "Oh, Katy, I've been so worried. When we left, I wasn't sure what would happen. Blake's threat to go to the cabin was too possible."

Kathryn tried to make light of it, as though it had been nothing at all. "I ain't seen hide nor hair of that varmint and if I did, well, I sleep with your big old gutting knife by my side." She thought this sounded very brave and woodsy, and then decided it also sounded prudent. She'd find a knife and put it by her bed the minute she returned to the cabin.

"You should go and stay at Kokum's. You'll be safe there."

Kathryn thought of the old woman, now so diminished. "Don't worry about me, Aunt Belle. I have to tell you something." She took a deep breath, then lowered her voice to a whisper, fearful of being overheard. "I know who the Highwayman is."

Her aunt's eyes went wide. *"Mon Dieu!* How did you find out?" she whispered back.

Kathryn dismissed this with a wave as though it were such an elementary deduction on her part that it wasn't worth mentioning. "Oh, the many disappearances, then showing up unannounced when he's needed, the midnight steed and his description – tall, ebony haired and handsome." She frowned. "Well, not my type of handsome, that's for sure. Each to her own, I always say. I must tell you, the lefty thing threw me, since he's a righty, but I thought that was part of his disguise."

Aunt Belle now appeared thoroughly confused. "What are you talking about, child?"

"Claude Remy...*Le Bandit de Grand Chemin*... The Highwayman! In his hero persona, he wears his knife on his left, denoting left-handedness, which Claude is not. As for *ebony-haired,* true, he has those white streaks, but most of his is dark enough. And the real giveaway was that time Claude said to tell you he had *'the goods';* then the Highwayman mysteriously delivers a pile of wonderful books on the doorstep..." She smiled smugly. "It wasn't hard to put two and two together."

Her aunt's mouth opened and closed like a fish out of water. "I think you need to do your arithmetic over again. Claude Remy is not the Highwayman!"

"Of course he is. I have it all worked out." Kathryn sniffed delicately.

"And *I* know for a fact that he is not. Remember who I was with last night. Claude was simply a good smoke-screen for the Spinster Tourond so I let things go along, knowing they would never go very far. Those other details are simply romanticized twaddle and could fit nearly any man in the province. As for *the goods* that Claude was bringing me.... He's a trapper, Katy – they were the *beaver pelts* I needed for Mrs. Prentiss' fancy coat."

Kathryn didn't know what to say. This made a mess of her brilliant deductions. "If Claude Remy isn't the High-wayman, who is?"

Aunt Belle's lips tightened before she spoke. "I can't tell you."

"You have to. He can go to Sergeant Prentiss and explain that you had nothing to do with the robbery."

"And then what? Do you really think they would believe him and we would both walk away? *Non, ma chère.* If I told you, there would simply be two ropes on the gallows."

The iron resolve in her aunt's voice let Kathryn know that was the only answer she'd get. She moved on. "I've been giving the robbery a lot of thought. I know the Highwayman didn't do it," here she looked to her aunt for confirmation and Belle nodded, "which means there's only one logical explanation. Constable Blake is the murderer." She continued laying out her case. "It makes sense. Blake arranged that he was on guard duty the night of the robbery. He kills Meltzer, the only witness, and then hides the money. Knowing the townspeople will demand blood for the murder of the guard, he sets things up so that the Highwayman, and now you, will take the fall and he'll get away scot-free." She paused; then added quickly, "All I have to do is prove it."

Her aunt readily agreed. "It makes terrible sense. Katy, you don't have much time. I heard Blake tell the sergeant they should move me to Lethbridge for trial in case the Highwayman tries to break me out of jail and that he will personally testify I was an accomplice in the murder of the guard."

Kathryn squeezed the cold metal bars on the cell door. "The one piece of evidence pinning this on the Highwayman is that knife. I *have* to get a look at it." A quick check confirmed that Sergeant Prentiss was still dutifully at his desk and that the constable's door remained open. "I'm going into his office. I'll leave the door to the cells open. If the Sergeant comes along, try to distract him. Wish me luck."

Her aunt reached through the bars, laying a protective hand on her niece's arm. "Please be careful, Kathryn."

The use of her name made Kathryn stop. She wrapped

her own hand firmly around her aunt's and felt Belle's tremble. "I will, and," she stood, straight and tall, "I prefer *Katy,* Katy Tourond, and I'm one of the Road Allowance People!"

She could still see the love and worry on her aunt's face, but now, there was pride too. "Everything's going to be fine, Aunt B." Kathryn assured her and mentally crossed all her fingers that it was true.

"By the way..." Her aunt eyed Kathryn's clothes. "That's a very familiar outfit. I have one exactly like it."

Kathryn managed to appear sheepish. "Actually, I borrowed it. You know, these trousers are very practical and comfortable, especially when riding old Nellie, and the coat is perfect. You should make me one."

Her aunt laughed, a sound that filled Kathryn's heart with hope.

"You, young lady, can make your own capote, as any self respecting Métis should."

Kathryn pressed her face against the bars and kissed her aunt on the cheek. Glancing at the back door leading to the alley, she got an idea. She moved to the door, opened it a crack, then took one of her hair pins and jammed it into the lock, preventing the striker from closing all the way and sealing the door.

Satisfied, Kathryn moved stealthily to the passageway to Constable Blake's office. Noiselessly, she slipped inside.

The late afternoon sun slanted through the fly-specked window, giving the room a wan light. Kathryn slid past the only chair in the room, noting the constable's coat hanging from the back. Hurrying to the cluttered desk, she swiftly rifled folders and pulled open drawers. Nothing. Then she spied a decrepit wooden filing cabinet pushed back into a dark corner. One of the scuffed drawers had a shiny padlock.

"Oh, really, Constable Dung? This place is like the bottom of an outhouse and you bother to put a new lock on your rubbish file cabinet? How unclever of you." She rummaged through the desk for the key without success, then as she shoved the papers aside on the impossibly messy top, Kathryn noticed an impression outlined on the desk blotter, as though there were something hard underneath. She lifted the edge of the green mat and almost cheered out loud.

A brass key glinted invitingly at her. Picking it up, she hurried to the filing cabinet and quickly opened the padlock.

"Eureka!" she whispered, and then looked down into the drawer. There was the knife. Its distinctive hilt carved with a wolf's head whose eerie eyes fairly gleamed in the fading light. It was Claude Remy's blade!

But – that didn't make sense.

And yet... She suddenly identified the peculiar smell lingering in the fetid air of Blake's office. It was the smell of brain-tanned leather. The smell of Claude Remy and his unforgettable coat!

Could it be? Was Claude mixed up in this after all?

Not as the Highwayman, but as...Cyrus Blake's *partner?*

"Impossible!" Kathryn breathed, but her mind raced. She remembered when Aunt Belle had been accosted by Blake in the alley. Her aunt had warned him that Claude was back from his trap lines and hinted that he was her protector. The constable had laughed and bragged, *"I'm not worried about that buck."* Any sensible man would be worried about tangling with Claude Remy, who was volatile and violent – two *v* words not to be ignored. What if Blake knew he didn't have to worry because *Claude was working for him?*

Unbelievable – yes. Incredible – absolutely. But disappointingly, it had to be true. Claude was Cyrus Blake's partner. Why, she couldn't guess, but they were in it together. It was an inside job with outside help – they had done the robbery together, and she bet Blake had promised the big woodsman a cut of the money for his part in the crime. Maybe he'd suggested Claude leave the knife so that it would seem like the Highwayman had done the murder. Everyone knew about the Highwayman and his distinctive white-handled dagger.

And then a darker thought crossed her mind. If Blake couldn't catch the actual Highwayman and wanted to hang the wild trapper instead, he could easily prove the knife with the wolf carving was Claude Remy's. With this knife, Blake owned Claude. The knife tied him to the murder and would ensure his silence.

Chapter 19

UNMASKED

Kathryn rode to the Thibault house hoping JP had been truthful when he said he knew everything about everybody. She was counting on it. She also hoped he'd forgiven her for what she had done.

He was in his usual tree, staring out at the sunset, when she rode up. She felt self-conscious as he watched her tie Nellie to the fence, then walk through the rustling grass to the base of the tree.

"Greetings, my liege." She reached out and traced the rough bark with her finger. "Are you speaking to me?"

JP's head dropped and at first she thought he was going to ignore her, and then she wondered if he was going to yell. Finally, she saw he was trying to hide a smile.

"It's hard to be angry at someone who draws disaster down like a lightning rod." He jumped out of the tree. "I hear you haven't exactly been successful in rallying yon troops."

Kathryn would have laughed if the situation hadn't been so dire. "You could say that." She watched him adjust his trademark hat. "I need your help, JP. You said you knew everything that happens in your kingdom. Was that the truth or were you simply trying to dazzle the local peasant girl?"

He laughed. "I know much more than I tell. It's safer that way."

She took a deep breath. "Do you know where Claude Remy has his cabin?"

This stopped him. "You mean out on his trap line?"

"Wherever you think he may be holed up."

"Perhaps. Why would you need that bushman?"

Kathryn knew the time had come to fill him in on everything. "Sit with me. I have a story and a daring plan to tell you."

JP took off his feathery chapeau and sat as she told him everything, including her suspicions.

"Kathryn, that's got a slim, closer to no, chance of working."

"Thanks for the vote of confidence. And, yes, it will work, but not unless Claude is there for the big reveal. So, we're back to my original question – can you find him?"

His disdain was almost comical. "Of course. He's got a cabin up by Beauvais Lake. Pretty rustic, even by River Falls' standards."

"JP, take me to him, please." She tried to stop the quiver in her voice. "I have to give him this." She withdrew the folded sheet of paper from her pant's pocket. "I have written a note to Monsieur Remy from that secret source of Métis justice we call The Highwayman, who knows all and tells few. Sound familiar?" She nudged JP with her elbow. "It tells Claude he must be at the barracks at ten o'clock tomorrow morning as Constable Blake has made plans to cut Claude out of his share." She yawned widely. "He'll know what that means."

"When was the last time you slept?" JP asked with more than a note of concern.

Kathryn heard something different in his voice, something older, more like a man than the boy she'd always thought him and it occurred to her that it had indeed been a long, long time since she'd had any rest. Like a mighty ocean wave, exhaustion washed over her. "As soon as we stealthily deliver the letter, I'll come back and hit the hay. Promise."

She struggled to her feet, stumbling, and JP hastily reached out to catch her, drawing Kathryn to him. He gently wiped a smudge of dirt from her face. "I'll make you a deal. You get some shut eye and I'll go play post-man to Claude Remy. He'll never catch me if I'm alone and to tell you the truth, I'm not sure your sleuthing skills are up to mine."

She ignored his tease and weighed whether she could indeed endure a trip to Beauvais Lake, wherever that was, then realized she was so tired, she could barely breathe. "You could take Nellie. She's a good horse."

JP smiled down at her, warm and real. "You go get her, and I'll tell my *maman* that I won't be home till late." He turned her around and gave her a small shove toward Nellie, who was busily feasting on Madame Thibault's lettuce.

Kathryn had barely managed to climb into the saddle when JP, wearing his signature hat and sporting a matching scarlet cape, bounded up and leapt onto Nellie, behind Kathryn. His arms skimmed past her waist and his hands covered hers on the reins.

"Let's go, old girl." He laughed as he gave the horse a light kick in the flanks. "And you too, Nellie!"

KATHRYN NEVER HEARD JP come back that night. In the morning she awoke early to find Nellie in her lean-to, safe and sound. The old mare had been fed, watered and given a brushing. There were some truly amazing people in the world and she knew at least two. The next time she saw him, Kathryn would tell JP he could borrow any book she had. Hastily dressing, she grabbed a bite of bannock from the breadbox and went back into her room.

Kathryn stood over her steamer trunk and gazed down into the neatly arranged case. It was still packed with all her clothes and belongings, ready to go as soon as she had the money to buy a ticket on the next train to Toronto.

But that was the old Kathryn's trunk.

Katydid had a whole new vision.

She pulled the clothes out and quickly tucked them in the low chiffonier which stood against the white-washed wall of her room. Next, to fill the space and give the trunk weight, she wedged in several pieces of wood crosswise, closed the lid and secured the hasp.

This had to appear real, which meant she needed to address the trunk. Try as she might, the only address she knew by heart was that of Our Lady of Mercy Academy for Young Ladies. In clear block letters, Kathryn wrote out the address, marking it *Attention: Sister Bernadette.* She hoped this gift of kindling would keep the blustery nun puzzling while she mumbled her rosary.

That done, she raced out to the lean-to and gave Nellie an extra cup of oats. "It's you and me to the rescue, Miss Nellie." She rubbed the mare's ears affectionately before going outside to the back of the shed and pulling the Phaeton into the yard. With much cursing, some in Michif which Kathryn was particularly proud of, she managed to hook Nellie to the rig. As though by magic, the old horse started to prance and nicker like a colt ready for a day in a green meadow after a long winter.

Then Kathryn hauled the trunk out and jammed it into the space behind the bench of the buggy. It didn't really fit and she used the safety belt to tie it down, hoping the heavy box didn't bounce loose and end up in splinters on the road. She was in a hurry.

The last thing she did was to go to her small library where she selected the novel *Ivanhoe.* Opening the cover, she extracted a thin envelope which contained the last of the money from her father's estate. She hoped that it would be enough.

Kathryn was about to put the volume back, then stopped. Her father had told her it was one of his favourites and that it always made him feel like a king in his castle home when he read it. She'd been saving this last gift from her father until she had a castle where she felt at home.

Looking around, Kathryn took stock of her tiny room, with the quite lovely iron bed and cheery rag rug on the floor, then the rest of the cabin, small and comfortable. The very definition of a home. It may not be the usual towering fortress of rock, but this was now her castle and she was very proud to be the valiant chevalier who would do battle for the fair Queen of River Falls, Mademoiselle Belle Tourond. She hugged the book to her chest, and then placed it carefully on her bedside table, ready to read.

Donning her aunt's capote, which she now considered the best apparel of all time, Kathryn raced back to the Phaeton and leapt into the seat. Grabbing the reins, she took a deep breath. The last time she'd held these, she'd almost killed both her and Aunt Belle. Now, she silently thanked her aunt for making her try to drive the buggy. She snapped the reins.

Nellie took off like a fresh three-year-old at the Kentucky Derby, but this time, Kathryn was ready for her. "That's enough! There's no time for this nonsense!" she shouted, and was amazed at the strength in her own voice. She sounded like Aunt Belle and Nellie responded by trotting as nice as you please, not a hoof out of place. Kathryn could have danced a jig. "That's it! Now we both know who's boss, there's no problem."

The early morning wind stung her eyes, then she saw the sunrise and it was glorious. The vibrant shades of pink and gold lifted her spirit with joy as the intoxicating smell of the wide-open prairie filled her lungs. This was wonderful country and she felt her heart open to it.

Kathryn wheeled into the Hopeful train station exhilarated with the new appreciation for the land she was now a part of. Leaping down from the Phaeton, she patted Nellie on the neck. "That was truly amazing, old girl. There'll be extra goodies in your feed bag tonight!"

After wrestling the trunk up the steps, she dragged it into the station and over to the counter.

"I need to ship this out, please."

The station master read the label and noted the sender's name. Instead of her own, Kathryn had written *Cyrus Blake.* He squinted at her over his thick glasses. His hair was a snow white halo around his head and the pipe sticking out of his pocket had left telltale traces of previous smoking sessions.

"Yes'm. I've seen you before, I believe."

Kathryn had no time for socializing, but didn't want to arouse suspicion. "Yes, I came in on the train a while back. About the trunk, I'm sending it for Constable Blake. He can't make it in right now."

He shot her a dubious look. "That's right neighbourly of you. Just the trunk? You're not going too?"

Kathryn didn't understand. "Me?"

"You're Katy Tourond, aren't you?"

"Yes." She didn't know where this was going.

"The same young lady who put up such a fuss when you arrived?"

Kathryn felt her cheeks flame at the memory of how she'd strutted around the station like some prima donna. He must have seen some of her antics. She cleared her throat. "That was a long time ago. I'm a lot older now."

"I remember your father when he was a young man..."

Kathryn tried to control her impatience, but time was ticking by.

The old station master went on. "A lot of the folks at River Falls thought it wrong when he went east and was passing. But some of us here in Hopeful understood. Being Métis isn't easy and life on the road allowances is harder still. Your pa was trying to make the best life possible for his family and did what he had to do to make that happen."

His deep brown eyes held hers for a long moment and understanding flowed between them.

"We all do what we must to protect our family," Kathryn agreed.

He nodded and then as she watched, he applied the documents which would send the trunk back to Toronto without her. A month ago, this would have made her sink into the depths of depression; now, she thought it a fitting way to break with the past and embrace her bright future.

"How much do I owe you?" Kathryn asked, opening the envelope with her precious few bills.

"Funny thing," he said with a nod. "Today's a special day. Freight goes for free."

Her surprise was written on her face. "Oh, thank you, and I need a receipt with the sender's name on it."

"I just bet you do," the station master laughed softly as he wrote out the document.

Kathryn climbed back onto the Phaeton and with only the merest hint from the reins, Nellie obligingly turned and struck out for Hopeful.

Chapter 20

HAPPILY EVER AFTER

Kathryn arrived in Hopeful as the bell at St. Michael's Church tolled ten o'clock. She tied Nellie up and was surprised to see a crowd of people in front of the jail. Sergeant Prentiss stood on the boardwalk, trying to calm the unruly mob.

"They killed Ed Meltzer, Sergeant!" One angry man called.

"She's as guilty as that no good Highwayman!" Another shouted.

"Bring her out here, we'll show her what we do with murdering half breeds!" A helpful citizen suggested.

Kathryn was disgusted and very frightened. What if this mob rioted and broke into the jail to get Aunt Belle?

Again the sergeant called for order. "You folks calm down. Nobody's doing anything crazy, you hear me?"

Avoiding the scene, Kathryn edged down the alley to the back door leading to the cells. She said a short prayer that the hair pin she'd jammed into the mechanism still held. As she turned the knob, she was rewarded as the back door opened and she saw Aunt Belle sitting on her pallet. Kathryn put her finger to her lips. "Where's Blake?" she mouthed.

Aunt Belle pointed toward the front of the building and whispered hoarsely. "At the window."

A trickle of sweat ran down her back as Kathryn stealthily made her way along the narrow hallway that led to the constable's office. It struck her that if Constable Dung was wearing his jacket, this whole plan could go up in smoke. This fear disappeared when she saw Blake, in his shirt and suspenders, peering out the front window, watching as his boss valiantly tried to control the angry crowd.

Why wasn't he out there supporting his fellow officer, she wondered, then realized how foolish the question was. Cyrus Blake wasn't about to put himself between a mob and Aunt Belle. Kathryn added *coward* to the long list of character flaws she'd assigned to the despicable constable.

In his office, she spied his greasy field jacket, still slung over the back of the chair. She slipped the shipping receipt with the station master's signature verifying the information into a pocket and then returned to the cells.

Aunt and niece exchanged conspiratorial smiles; then Kathryn left the jail, carefully removing the hair pin from the lock as she went.

As she walked around to the front of the building, she could hear the clamour of voices and it was much louder than before. Kathryn stood at the back of the angry mob and had never felt so alone. Scanning the crowd, she prayed JP had been successful and that Claude had taken the bait.

There was the jarring sound of shattering glass as a rock was hurled through the window of the jail.

Sergeant Prentiss cursed as he saw his constable standing behind the broken window. "Cyrus, get out here, man!"

Kathryn knew the constable well enough by now that she was sure he would put on his jacket, the one vestige of authority he had, before venturing out.

Sure enough, moments later, he emerged clad in the jacket now with a grubby lanyard hanging limply, and swaggered forward like he was the salvation of the sergeant and a gift to humanity.

Kathryn knew the moment had come. The lives of her aunt and the Highwayman hung in the balance. Taking a steadying breath, she called out. "Sergeant Prentiss! I need to talk to you."

The crowd turned to stare and she heard a couple of men mutter *half-breed* and *road allowance trash*. Pushing rudely past a disgruntled gentleman in a long coat and fancy hat, Kathryn forced her way to the front, then faced the crowd.

"My name is Kathryn Tourond. My Aunt Belle had nothing to do with this robbery and murder and more than that, the Highwayman is innocent of the charges as well!"

The mob fell silent, and then a man's voice was heard. "Yeah, if you believe that, then I'm King Edward."

There was laughing as another voice added, "What a surprise, a dirty breed sticking up for another dirty breed."

Sergeant Prentiss motioned for the crowd to be quiet. "Kathryn, I know you want your aunt to be free. What you need to remember is Constable Blake has proof the Highwayman did this crime and Belle was caught consorting with the outlaw."

"That squatter is guilty as sin and she'll pay with her neck!" This suggestion brought resounding approval.

"I know who stole that money!" Kathryn shouted over the tumult.

Constable Blake glared at her. The malice in his face was frightening and Kathryn felt her knees weaken.

Sergeant Prentiss was genuinely interested now. "Everyone is innocent until proven guilty, Kathryn, and that includes Belle. If you have new information, I need it. Who is this thief?"

She swallowed, then straightened her spine and spoke in a clear, strong voice. "Constable Cyrus Blake stole that bank money and framed the Highwayman so that he would take the blame."

Blake snapped forward like a striking cobra. "You lying little half breed!"

Pandemonium broke out and several people jostled Kathryn, one man with yellowed teeth shoved her backward and she almost fell.

Sergeant Prentiss motioned for silence. "Cyrus was a

friend to Edward Meltzer, Kathryn. He came in on his day off to help Ed guard the payroll. And we have hard evidence; we have the knife belonging to the Highwayman." His voice was calm and reasonable, almost agreeable, but she could hear the scepticism in it.

Cyrus Blake wasn't about to let her accuse him. "I got the blade, alright, and I think this thievin' squatter should see it." He stormed back into the jail and returned seconds later with the knife which he held up for the crowd to see. "Still stained with an innocent man's blood!" he shouted, and the crowd howled.

"That's not the Highwayman's knife!" Kathryn protested. "Blake is a murderer or is an accomplice to murder. He most certainly masterminded the theft."

Sergeant Prentiss took the knife from Blake and shook his head sadly. "Ed was a good man."

This was not going as Kathryn planned. She scanned the faces in the crowd and saw that no one believed her, worse; she now heard several voices saying that she was probably in on it too and should be thrown into jail along with her aunt.

A gasp rose from the back of the crowd, then a murmur that increased in volume. Kathryn peered over the heads of the onlookers.

Striding jauntily down the street, a red chapeau with a shiny black feather bobbed toward the crowd. The hat sat atop a smiling young man with eyes that twinkled at her.

It was her Prairie Puss-in-Boots and he wasn't alone.

With him was Madame Ducharme, old Kokum, leaning on her cane, and walking proudly beside her was a tall, raven-haired and extremely handsome man Kathryn had never seen before. He was dressed in black and on his left hip was an ivory handled knife for all to see. One arm had a bandage and Kathryn remembered the shot that had been fired when the rendezvous had been raided.

Behind this vanguard was a large parade of people. Some Kathryn knew and they all appeared extremely determined. There was Pierre and Francis, with Joseph striding beside them. Next came Madame Garnier and her husband along with JP's mother and her brood of boys tagging behind. A thin man with bright red hair sticking out from his head had to be Henri Beauchamp, and with him was a tiny black-haired woman and eight young children, half with carrot hair and half with their mother's black braids.

All the Métis in the district must have come and Kathryn wondered what had changed their minds. And more surprising was that in the crowd, she recognised some citizens of Hopeful, white citizens, including Mr. and Mrs. Jones, proudly carrying baby Louisa who waved a chubby arm to the crowd. Then she saw JP's triumphant face and she knew who the silver-tongued persuader had been.

The parade stopped as Kokum stamped her cane on the street, sending up a tiny cloud of fine silvery dust. "We're here to demand justice. Belle Tourond is innocent as is my son," she laid a loving hand on the tall stranger's arm, "Gabriel Ducharme, whom you know as The Highwayman."

A murmur swept through the crowd as everyone talked at once.

"There's your murderer and thief, Sergeant!" Constable Blake pointed an accusing finger at Gabriel Ducharme.

The venom in Blake's tone was easy to hear and Kathryn remembered how the constable had lost his ear.

The tall stranger stepped forward. "I am the Highwayman. I am also *not* the one responsible for the bank robbery or murder of that guard." He went on in his own defence. "I was forced to act under cover of darkness as I knew the Métis rights were being trampled and they would get no help from the law." Here Sergeant Prentiss had the decency to look ashamed. "I also knew that Constable Blake would try again to kill me if it were known that his first attempt, when he shot me in the back, had been unsuccessful. I had to stay hidden so that I could continue to help my people."

The sergeant's calculating gaze took in the wounded stranger. "We have proof that it was the Highwayman committed the robbery and killed the guard in cold blood: eyewitness testimony from Constable Blake – and this murder weapon." He showed the stranger the knife with its fancy antler handle.

Gabriel removed his own knife from its sheath and held it up. "And yet, Sergeant, I still have my knife with a true ivory hilt. Ivory is a rare commodity, and I have never seen a second blade like this."

The sergeant mulled this over. "You know, I've never seen one either...before today." He shot Blake an inquiring look, but the constable only scowled back.

"And there is another reason I could not have committed that crime, Sergeant Prentiss." The man Kathryn now knew was Gabriel Ducharme continued. "On the night of the robbery, I was with Belle Tourond. She can verify this."

"We'd best get Belle out here, Cyrus. Go fetch her from the cells."

Reluctantly, the constable disappeared into the jail and appeared moments later gripping Aunt Belle by the arm.

He shoved her forward and even from where she stood, Kathryn could see the angry red welt where his fist had been.

"Belle, this man," the sergeant tipped his head toward Gabriel, "says you and he were together the night of the robbery. Is that true?"

Kathryn saw her aunt's face light up when she saw Gabriel. "Yes, Sergeant, we were."

"I don't mean to be indelicate, Belle, but was he with you all night?"

Belle blushed prettily. "Until dawn."

"She's lying to protect her buck," Cyrus Blake scoffed.

"It's true," Gabriel stepped forward. "We have a witness, at least for part of the night: Father Blanchet, who married us at midnight in St. Michael's Church."

This revelation sent more waves through the crowd.

The sergeant took his Stetson off and wiped his forehead with his sleeve. "Well, that does put a fine edge on things."

Kathryn was stunned. Aunt Belle married! To this stranger, this.... She watched the two of them, love written on their faces and her heart went out to them.... This *Bandit du Grand Chemin*, this Highwayman. She felt giddy. Her aunt beamed at her as she blew Kathryn a kiss.

Kathryn remembered the sleeping draught her aunt had given her the night of the robbery and wondered if there had been another brew, maybe in the tea, to give her the headache in the first place.

Then a conversation she'd had with her aunt came into Kathryn's head in which Aunt Belle made reference to *her Gabe* as though he were still alive. *He is the best man she'd ever met* and how *she cherishes every moment with him* and they *have a destiny together*. That's what had clanged – the tenses were wrong – present instead of past. Although it had struck her as strange at the time, in the light of the man's miraculous resurrection, it made perfect sense.

Aunt Belle and the mysterious Highwayman were a

fairytale right out of one of her books. It was perfect – except for one little detail. The real thief had yet to be exposed. They weren't home and dry yet. Kathryn needed to finish what she started. "Sergeant Prentiss, there is proof that the Highwayman, I mean, Monsieur Ducharme, did not commit the robbery." Her voice was barely heard above the noise.

JP shouldered his way through the mob of town's people and stood beside Kathryn. He then stuck two fingers in his mouth a let out an ear-piercing whistle. There was immediate silence.

"Much better," he said as together he and Kathryn faced the sergeant.

Kathryn prayed her plan would work. An old expression danced in her head: *the end justifies the means.* She knew the ending she wanted would require some devious means and what she was about to do was about as devious as one could get.

"I believe that Constable Blake stole the money. He is currently shipping it out of Hopeful on the noon train. The constable is sending it back east where he will take up a lavish residence and live the privileged life of a wealthy gentleman after he has made sure the wrong people pay for his crime and the case is closed." Even to her, it sounded scandalous.

Blake scoffed. "That's a lot of talk, except I don't see no proof."

"Check his pockets, Sergeant. Since it was sent this

morning, I'm sure there must be an official document, signed by the station master, showing he shipped one large trunk of sufficient size to hold the entire payroll, to Toronto. His name is probably written on it."

The crowd now waited, curious.

Sergeant Prentiss turned to his constable. "Let's settle this right now, Cyrus."

"Dang it, Sergeant, you ain't going to listen to that, that..."

"That *young lady,* Cyrus? Yes I am. Empty your pockets. That's an order."

Cursing, Constable Blake turned the pockets on his breeches inside out showing they were empty.

Kathryn watched his expression and couldn't decide whether it was self-righteousness or arrogance; either way, he was mighty sure of himself. Then as he fumbled in his jacket, this sureness evaporated and his face went a startling shade of puce. Slowly, he withdrew a neatly folded slip of paper.

He stared down at it, as though it was a rattlesnake nestled in his palm.

Sergeant Prentiss took the paper and read it. "It's as Kathryn said. This is a way bill for the shipping of a trunk to Toronto, Ontario, and your name is listed as the shipper, Cyrus. Care to explain?"

Before the constable could say anything, there was a sudden roar from the direction of the alley as a mountain of a man bellowed and lumbered toward the barracks.

"Swindler! Liar! *Cochon!*" The crowd parted as Claude Remy bulled his way through. "You stole dat money from da bank and now you tink you can steal my share from me! It was you who stabbed dat guard, den you kept my knife so we could blame da Highwayman." He eyed Gabriel Ducharme. "I do not tink dat trick she be working today." Lunging toward Blake, he made a grab for the terrified constable. "I tear off your head and spit in da hole..."

Kathryn took an involuntary step backward, although whether it was from fright or to allow Claude clear access to his target, she couldn't say.

Sergeant Prentiss suddenly held his pistol. "No one's doing anything until I have a chance to straighten this mess out. What in the Sam Hill is going on here?"

Claude froze. "I did dis for you, Belle, *ma chère.*" He looked at Belle, longing in his eyes. "I thought if Gabriel, he was out of da way, your heart would soften toward me, dat's why I told Blake dat Gabe was in Medicine Hat. It was to be a secret, but da pig, he blackmailed me into help- ing him wid da robbery. If I didn't, he would tell you how he knew where Gabriel was and you would hate me. The money, it give us a new start together, far from dis town. I wouldn't have to spend my life on da trap line and we could be married."

Kathryn watched her aunt recoil. "Claude, you betrayed Gabriel..., your people..." She shook her head sadly, "And me...for nothing. It would never have happened. We would never have married. I am so sorry."

She looked toward Gabriel and Kathryn could practically feel the love her aunt shared with this stranger, her Highwayman. It was better than any theatrical production she had ever seen. It was romantic, mysterious, tragic and uplifting all at the same time. At moments like this, Kathryn wished she were a playwright like Shakespeare perhaps, so that she could pen this immortal love story for future generations to read and weep over.

Her attention was abruptly pulled back to the drama unfolding in front of her when Sergeant Prentiss raised his pistol and pointed it at Blake. "You're under arrest Cyrus, and so is this friend of yours." He motioned both men into the detachment. "Gabe, I'll deal with you later. I need more answers and there's the matter of some missing goods you forgot to pay for."

Kathryn could hear Claude cursing in every language he knew as he was hustled back to the cells.

In a heartbeat, Gabriel was on the boardwalk and had taken Belle into his arms. Kathryn watched as enthralled as when reading a particularly wonderful passage in one of her books. It was *très romantique!*

Belle wrapped her arms around her new husband; then, to the cheers of the crowd, the couple kissed. Everyone began talking and exclaiming over the extraordinary events of the morning.

JP shook his head. "I must admit, I didn't see that one coming. I knew Gabe was back and was our Highwayman, but I sure couldn't say anything. Kokum and Belle would both have killed me. It was the best kept secret in River Falls."

"Now they know you can keep a secret." She said, then added with a smile, "at least if it involves bodily harm to your person, my liege."

Reaching up, he smoothed back the feather on his hat with two fingers. "I do have a question. How did you know Claude would confess to the robbery?"

Kathryn folded her arms. "Because I'm such an astute judge of character." Then she giggled. "And after dealing with Claude, I knew he would explode with the right encouragement. I had the feeling that he and Constable Dung had an unknown history and that his hatred had been festering for some time."

"I could have told you Claude Remy was dangerous. Our trapper has fists like ham hocks and I've seen him use them, from a safe distance mind you," JP added.

"Plus, despite appearances, Claude is not a stupid man. He would know that with Blake holding his knife, he would always be under the man's control and was probably expecting his partner to cheat him." Kathryn grew pensive. "And you know what? I'm sure the good constable would indeed have swindled Claude out of his share. What could a Métis do if a North West Mounted Police constable accused him of a crime? Blake may even have implicated him with the Highwayman. After all, he had that blasted knife – kind of two birds with one stone. It makes sense. I simply sped up the double-cross."

"I think you're right," JP agreed as he and Kathryn strolled across the street away from the crowd. "You've been through a lot since joining our little kingdom – discovering you were Métis, living as a member of the Road Allowance People, unmasking a Canadian Robin Hood, bringing a murderer to justice and – let's not forget – wearing dungarees!"

Kathryn beamed into his wonderful face. "As I've said before – some rewards are worth the struggle."

"And speaking of rewards, tell me, Kathryn the Great, will you go back to your home with the reward money the bank has offered?" he asked tentatively.

This was one detail that had slipped her mind. Now she felt a little lightheaded as she realized what it meant. She had five thousand dollars! She had the means to go back to Toronto, pay for law school and live comfortably ever after. She could leave River Falls and these Outcasts far behind.

"I will go to law school in the east..." She saw his face fill with sadness. "However," she hurried on, "my home... and my heart, are here now JP. I will always come back to River Falls."

Kathryn saw the relief sweep through him and laughed. "Someone must stand up for these people's rights and who better than a Métis lady lawyer."

It had been an eventful time. She remembered when she'd first seen the town and had decided it was more Hopeless than Hopeful, but now, with everyone talking and laughing, Road Allowance People with white, she decided Hopeful was a good name after all. Her aunt had said they must plant the seeds and wait for the harvest. Watching all these happy folks, Kathryn was hoping for a bumper crop.

It was a start.

She would always love her stories of knights and damsels in distress but she now knew life was not a fairy tale; it was hard work and took a special kind of courage to stand up and do the right thing. She thought of Mark and his threat to run the Road Allowance People off so he could set up his hog operation. If she were going to help these people, no, *her* people, she would need that special courage and Kathryn knew she had it. Clara Brett Martin would be very proud of her, and she realized, so would her parents.

However, she wasn't about to close the covers on her fairytale books entirely. When she was with her Prairie Puss-in-Boots, she would always share that rare realm of magic that had brought them together. She smiled impishly. "As a reward for finding the true villainous Black Knights of this tale, will you grant me a boon, sire?"

"For the fairest maiden in all the land, anything." JP

took off his hat and with a grand flourish, bowed deeply, ready to jump into the game once more.

"Will you please, please tell me what *JP* stands for?"

He hesitated, balking. "Oh, fair lady, me thinkest that thou knoweth how I feel about that one secret." Then his face softened in surrender. Reaching out, he took her hands in his, drawing her to him.

He was so close; Kathryn could feel the heat of his body. Her heart sped up and she felt a distinct tingling sensation. Leaning in, he whispered into her ear.

Kathryn's eyes went wide, then, as naturally as if she'd done it a thousand times, her lips brushed his. "Impossible!"

AUTHOR'S NOTE

This story really starts when Métis combatants were defeated by the Canadian government in a four-day battle in May of 1885 at Batoche, Saskatchewan. This just fight – the Métis were defending their rights, land and culture – is known as the North West Resistance and was led by Louis Riel and Gabriel Dumont. You can read more about it (and about Aunt Belle's youth) in my book, *Belle of Batoche.*

After this pivotal event in history, the Métis were considered traitors and renegades, and the era of the great dispersal began. Some, whose skin was light-coloured, passed as white, burying their ancestry in order to survive. Others, whose First Nations roots were obvious, went back to the trap lines of the north.

Here in Western Canada, prejudice against non-whites meant they couldn't live in towns and as they were not Status Indian, they were not allowed to live on reserves. Many Métis had no choice but to live on unused government land adjacent to the roadways and became known as the Road Allowance People. These stalwart souls strove to preserve their culture and very existence against harsh odds and slim chances, trying to survive while maintaining the positive Métis spirit of family and community. They had had their fight and lost; so, they accepted this treatment, however unfair it was, until 1945, when conditions improved and the Métis were no longer on the fringes of society.

The Métis nation is a distinct ethnicity and has been in existence since the beginning of the fur trade, when white European trappers from French Canada, England, Ireland and Scotland took First Nation's wives. The children of these unions were the first Métis in Canada.

The Métis do not live on reserves, although there are eight Settlements in Alberta – communities in which some families have chosen to make their homes. The Métis have their own language, called Michif, which consists of French nouns and Cree verbs; and, the Métis people had their own flag before Canada did – more than a hundred fifty years before. The Métis Infinity, or Circle of Eight, flag shows a white infinity sign against either a red or blue background. It too has its roots in the fur trade, as it was given to the Métis by Alexander MacDonnell, a North West Company agent.

Today, the Métis people are a thriving and vital part of Canadian society, contributing in all professions and walks of life, but you would be hard pressed to pick one out of a crowd. You may be sitting next to a Métis person right now!

Jacqueline Guest
Bragg Creek, Alberta, 2011
www.jacquelineguest.com

ACKNOWLEDGEMENTS

The author would like to thank the host of people who contributed their expertise, memories and advice which were so valuable in the writing of this book.

The following is a partial list of these helpful souls: Nik Burton, Coteau Books; Laura Peetoom, Paperglyphs Editorial; Darren Prefontaine, Gabriel Dumont Institute; Lorain Lounsberry, Glenbow Museum; Wendy Kraushaar, RCMP Historical Collections Unit, Depot Division; Tri River Métis Elders and Youth Group; The Tourond Family; Margaret Tourond Townson; Marguerite Harrison; Saskatchewan Archives Board.

Verifying oral history is extremely difficult, but by combining fact with fiction, I tried to make this book both historically correct, as well as, an entertaining read for young people.

I would also like to recognize the Canada Council for the Arts. Your generous support allowed me to take the extensive blocks of time necessary to write this important novel.

Thank you!

ABOUT THE AUTHOR

Jacqueline Guest is the author of more than sixteen books for young readers, specializing in sports themes, teen mysteries or historical fiction. Her books have received numerous Our Choice and Young Readers Choice citations. Jacqueline Guest lives and writes in the Rocky Mountain foothills of Alberta.

FSC
www.fsc.org

MIX

Paper from
responsible sources

FSC® C016245

Printed in Canada at Friesens